GIRLS AND BOYS COME OUT TO PLAY

A Christmas Ghost Story

A Novella

RICHARD SAVIN

For my great friends David and Jamie

Next stop Hollywood

The moral right of the author has been asserted.

Apart from any fair dealing for the purposes of research or private study, or criticism or review, as permitted under the Copyright, Designs and Patents Act 1988, this publication may only be reproduced, stored or transmitted, in any form or by any means, with the prior permission in writing of the publishers, or in the case of reprographic reproduction in accordance with the terms of licences issued by the Copyright Licensing Agency. Enquiries concerning reproduction outside those terms should be sent to the publishers.

This is a work of fiction. Names, characters, businesses, places, events and incidents are either the products of the author's imagination or used in a fictitious manner. Any resemblance to actual persons, living or dead, or actual events is purely coincidental.

© Richard Savin 2019

ACKNOWLEGEMENTS

My thanks to David Povilaitis for endless patience and invaluable assistance with the cover design. To Liz for the editorial guidance and of course my beta readers. Thanks also to the VEEM Writers Group for encouragement and comment.

THE RHYME

Sung to the tune of the 18th century nursery rhyme
"Boys and girls come out to play"

Following, following always to roam
Following, following leaving your home
Follow the music that leads you away
Hoping you'll come back one happy day

Climb up the stairs and into your bed
Pull up the blanket and over your head
Don't hark to the music or you will be led
To the place where you stay until you be dead

Following, following, list'ning too long
Following, following, things do go wrong
Over the marshes and far, far away
Maybe you'll come back one happy day.

Don't follow the music, don't follow the sound
Stay safe in your bed till the morn' comes around
Don't follow the piper for he'll make you pay
And you'll never come home though your mother's do pray.

Prologue

Somewhere in the distance a dog was barking; a hollow insistent bark that drifted across the landscape and lost itself in the horizon.

Closer, along the riverbank, there were voices; anxious, distressed voices touched by a cold feeling of apprehension at what they might not hear back.

They called out into the frost-bitten air in a vain chorus and waited on the reply they knew, deep in their hearts, would not come.

A small dinghy with an outboard motor stuttered out on the slack water. The tide had completed its ebb and as the tiny craft trawled back and forth on what was left of the water, the landscape around it was a sea of mud. The man at its tiller could be seen peering into the muddy shallows, looking for what he hoped he would not see.

Further away, out on the marshes, the undefined images of men could be seen fanned out in a thin line, picking their way carefully across the boggy swamp of reeds and mud. They chose their path, cautiously putting their feet down on the root clumps, testing each step with the pressure of a boot, ever conscious of the thick fathomless mud that surrounded them; mud that with a fall would suck its victim into a dark liquid embrace, an embrace from which there was little chance of rescue. As hard as a man might pull, the mud could pull back harder; it would never let go of its prize – whoever fell would be beyond help.

The winter afternoon was beginning to darken and a thin mist was coming up. They had been out since a watery sun had risen that morning, calling and shouting, combing through the matted grass that lined the river bank – grass that was stiff with frost and crunched underfoot. Soon the light would be gone and they would be forced to give up the search.

It was almost dark when a far cry came to them.

In twos and threes the men returned, ferried across the river in the dinghy to where the others waited, their breath bated in paralysed anticipation of what they did not wish to hear.

One of the men held out an object. They had found a glove, a solitary grey woollen glove. In the cold of the dark air there was the sound of someone sobbing.

The Christmas of 1920 would not be a happy one.

CHAPTER 1

The snow

1927. It was going to be a white Christmas; he could feel it on the air: that crisp, slightly spangled sensation. It came with the little sprays of gold stardust picked up in the headlights.

He was approaching Norwich when the first flutter of paper-like flakes began to twist towards the windscreen. He mentally crossed his fingers that it wouldn't snow too hard, then turned up the heater so that it blew hot dry air against the screen.

As he entered the city the snow began to settle, thinly at first but the flakes were getting bigger, fatter and more lush as they tumbled in the silver beam of the headlights, like plump, grey bees swirling in a dervish dance.

In the city the lights on Christmas trees peeked out of windows at him, tucked away in warm rooms with welcoming fires burning in open hearths. He caught the smell of wood smoke, and hints of roasting chestnuts that spiced the night air, infusing it with a deep sense of the festivity to come. It was three days to Christmas Eve.

There was very little out on the roads. He passed a horse and cart laden with barrels, labouring slowly to wherever it was bound, but it was an odd hour for a brewers' drayman to be abroad.

By the time he left the last of the old-fashioned gas lamps behind, those not yet replaced by the new modern electric lights, the snow on the ground had thickened and he could feel it scrunch as it compressed under the car's tyres.

On the outskirts of the city he picked up the sign that pointed to Great Yarmouth. Not far now, he comforted himself.

A few miles on and the snow was beginning to pack under the windscreen wipers and when he reached the point where the Acle road made its way across the open marshland, he finally had to stop; he would have to get out and clear it. It was less than five miles to

Great Yarmouth and from there only another three to his destination, Breydon Hall.

Standing next to the car with the bonnet steaming and melted snow dribbling off its curved scuttle, the air seemed surreally enchanted; the only sounds, the quiet, contented tick-over of the engine and the squeak of the snow under his boot as he stepped out onto it. There was no wind and the covering of snow muted everything to a silent stillness, like a great marzipan and icing blanket. It felt like he was perched on the top of a Christmas cake.

For a moment he stood motionless, taking in the silence, mesmerised by the gently drifting flakes falling about him. He took a deep breath then shook himself of out his watching trance. A stream of condensation fogged out of his mouth like a fire-breathing dragon. He got the leather fingers of his driving gauntlets under the windscreen wipers and slid away the slabs of snow that had compressed into ice underneath the blades.

Back in the warmth of the car he spread a tartan travel blanket across his knees, selected first gear and, with the back wheels slipping a little, he moved on.

As he reached the outer edge of Great Yarmouth the sense that greeted him was quite removed from that of the season. The houses were poor; terraced and back-to-back they huddled together like cold, unfed children. Their lights were dim, with wavering candles and flickering oil lamps; there were none of the colours of Christmas, the greens, the reds, the golds and the silvers that had peeped out at him from the homes of Norwich. Here, instead, there was a strong smell of fish and fish smoking, of herring guts and bloaters. It was the home of the North Sea fishing fleet and the herring was the master.

By the time he passed the dark shadow of Vauxhall station, the snowfall had thinned and then finally fluttered to a stop. Driving away from the town he encountered a bus grinding along Southtown Road, the light inside looking incongruously jolly as it spilled out onto the whiteness, its passengers all huddled and swaddled in thick coats and scarves.

At the town of Gorleston he turned right and pointed the long bonnet of the car towards the village of Breydon and the sanctuary of his hosts.

The sign on the outskirts of the village was overlapped with snow and barely readable. The narrow road that ran through it had no pavements, just grass verges that were now smudged and indistinct under a layer of white. Only the cottages and their paling fences, jutting up like sentinel spears, marked out where the road was hidden.

The village was marshalled around a square, punctuated at its centre by a newly constructed memorial to those who had not returned from the Great War: a forlorn stone soldier, head bowed, hands resting on the butt of an upturned rifle, its bayonet stabbed into the ground. The effigy stood cold and cheerless except for a garland of holly and tinsel that someone had hung around its neck, the colours glittering in the light flowing out of the pub which flanked one side of the square. Coming from inside he heard the muted sound of a piano being played and voices singing; he thought he vaguely recognised a Christmas tune but he couldn't be sure.

On the opposing side of the square the church sat in contrasting darkness. It was around seven o'clock and he guessed that they had already had an early service and there would not be another until the festive Evensong.

He left the square and drove along the road which ran across the Breydon marshes. Breydon Hall was on the far side of the village, perched on the edge of a swampy expanse known as Breydon Water. It was not a lake but rather an estuarial lagoon of salt water which formed the confluence of three rivers: the Waveney, Yare and Breydon. The marshy swamplands surrounding it were home to the bittern, a local variety of rare brown heron, and this is what he had come for. James Astley was an amateur ornithologist and wading birds were his particular interest.

Brigadier Sir Anthony Boyes, the owner of Breydon Hall, had been a friend of Astley's father; they had served together in the Sudan when General Gordon had been slaughtered at Khartoum and they had survived under fire in the Boer Wars. His father was now dead from a motoring accident. He was not well acquainted with the Brigadier, having not seen him or Breydon since he was ten. He had written to them earlier in the year asking if he might join them for the holiday and at first there had been a reluctance. So when the invitation had finally come to spend Christmas at the Hall it was one he enthusiastically accepted. The opportunity to catch sight of, and perhaps photograph, the shy bittern was too good to miss.

A bit before the lane which led to the Hall, just as he was passing the last of the string of cottages on the outskirts, a shadow fled without warning from out of nowhere and into the path of the car. He swerved, the car slid sideways and there was the sickening thump of a human body hitting the coachwork. The car slithered to a halt and he was immediately out onto the snow, his boots crunching towards where the figure of a child lay motionless on the ground. As he ran towards it two more figures emerged from one of the cottages: a man and a woman. The woman was screaming in a voice edged with terror. They both knelt at the side of the child who now showed signs of recovery. As he reached them he could see that the victim was a small girl, probably no more than five or six years old, clad only in a nightdress and clutching a small doll in one hand. The man scooped her up in his arms and the child, though dazed, began to struggle and moan. The man held her tightly to his chest.

'I'm most dreadfully sorry,' Astley said, horrified and at a loss for anything more to say. He looked at the child with mild relief on seeing that she was alive and, apart from the shock, seemed unharmed. He had not actually run her down; instead, as he swerved, she had run into the side of the car and had been thrown backwards onto the ground. Now she appeared no more than distressed by the event; the thick layer of snow had probably saved her from more serious injury.

Astley stood there for a moment, looking from one parent to the other. He could find nothing to say other than repeating how sorry and devastated he was. The woman, however, responded strangely. She pressed her hands on his, clasping them like a supplicant and, through what looked like tears of relief, she thanked him.

'Oh sir,' she whimpered, 'oh sir, oh sir, how can I thank you?'

James Astley was confused by the behaviour and at first put it down to shock and the elation that the child was not dead, but then the man, still clutching the now shivering child, began to react in the same fashion, profusely showering him with almost abject apologies and heartfelt thanks. Astley stood there, unsure of what to do or say, but the position was resolved for him as the couple retreated, with little bows and further thanks, back into their cottage.

He stood for a while in the silence of the night still trying to fathom the depths of what had transpired but unable to make any sense of it. When he got back to the car and was about to get in he thought he heard a sound, then he caught it: a plaintive voice of someone singing, probably in one of the cottages. It was not a song he recognised but it had a lilting and pleasant melody and, although he could not catch the words, the tune stayed with him and he found himself whistling it as he drove the final short distance to Breydon Hall.

He turned in through the gates and the scrunch of the gravel under his wheels alerted a dog and caused it to bark. As he got out of the car the solid oak door of the hall opened and a flood of electric light gushed out. Another lamp, over the front porch, was illuminated and from inside the hallway he was greeted by a well-dressed tree hung with brightly coloured baubles, carefully wrapped gift boxes and small shimmering lights.

'Welcome, welcome, dear boy.' The Brigadier stood framed and smiling in the arched doorway with an outstretched hand. 'I've had a generator installed, pretty good show don't ya think?' He waved an arm expansively around the display of electricity. 'It's the electric age don'tcha know, my boy. We're all modern here now – no more smelly old paraffin oil or smoky candles. Hah, come in, come in, I'll get Parky to bring yer things in. Come along.'

CHAPTER 2

Poachers

'When you've had a chance for a wash and brush-up I'll see you in the drawing room. Pamela will pour you a sherry – if that's to yer taste, that is.' The Brigadier followed it up with a chortling laugh.

Astley climbed the broad staircase which led to a galleried landing above. He climbed past heavily gilded frames, out from which the rigid images of moustachioed and uniformed ancestors stared down, hollow-eyed men whose sombre gaze seemed to follow his progress. He crossed the landing to a corridor that was lined with more ancestors, this time the women of the tribe. He paused for a moment and glanced at one of them. She looked pale, he thought, pale and not in terribly good health. The eyes were sad; all the eyes were sad and all the faces were pale.

Shortly after he found his room there was a knock on the door. A short, thin man in his late middle-age brought in his bags. 'I'm Parkinson, sir,' he said cheerfully, 'Brigadier's batman. Been with his lordship on every campaign, including the last one against the Hun.'

He pointed towards the bed where the covers had been turned down. 'Mrs M the housekeeper's aired it for you, sir. I hope you'll be comfortable.' With that he gave a sort of salute and reversed out into the corridor.

The room had an electric light hung on a flex from a rose in the ceiling. There was a brass switch on the wall by the door. Next to the bed on a marble-topped table there was another lamp, this one with a Lalique glazed shade in the modern Art Deco style. It was heated by a cast iron radiator, which clearly owed its origins to a recent installation, and this made the room comfortably warm. A Tudor casement window let onto the front drive of the house and the countryside beyond.

He stood for a moment in the shallow bay and, pressing his face close to the leaded glass panes, tried to peer out into the night but the glare from the electric lamps behind him rendered it impossible. He crossed the room and switched them off then returned to the window and this time opened it. A rush of dark frosted air struck his skin and caused it to prickle with small goose bumps. For a moment or two he stood looking out at the white-coated scene. He could just make out the fretted line of tall reeds and there was now a moon that lit the surface of Breydon Water. He lingered for a moment, contemplating the thought that somewhere out there the bitterns would be silently roosting.

The cold began to penetrate his chest and he decided it was best to close the window. Tomorrow he would get out his binoculars and place a chair in the bay. From that vantage point he could search the near marshes for signs of the birds. Later he thought he might take a boat and row across to where he could get in among the reeds. As he pulled the window shut his ear caught a sound and he hesitated. It was that tune again, and it brought him back to the incident with the child. He pushed open the casement and put his head back out into the night, straining his ears to catch the sounds. It was a woman's voice or maybe that of a young boy soprano, but he could see no one and after a brief moment it had gone. He pulled the window shut, fastened it and drew the heavy drapes across the bay.

Turning on the lights again, he set to and changed out of his travelling clothes. He pulled on a fair isle sweater and then a tweed sports jacket. Suitably dressed, he went down the stairs to the drawing room where the Brigadier and his wife, Lady Pamela Boyes, were sitting in comfortable leather chairs facing a cheerful log fire that burned brightly in a generous inglenook hearth. The mantelpiece was draped in a garland of holly woven together with strands of ivy and studded with red, silver and blue glass baubles. In one corner there was a tall Christmas tree, alive with miniature electric lights and draped with ribbons of silver tinsel like glittering feather boas. It stood in a tub around which red crepe paper had been wound. Against its base were piled brightly wrapped packages and boxes, presents for the family and guests.

The Brigadier and Pamela both stood up. 'James,' Pamela came over to him and put a hand on his arm. She smiled warmly. 'So nice to have you here, my but you've grown. The last time I saw you, you were just so high,' and she put out a hand at about the level of his waist.

Astley smiled, 'Yes, I think I was ten at the time, Aunt Pamela.'

The Brigadier laughed. 'No need to be so formal, my boy. Call us Anthony and Pamela. We're all grown-ups together, what.'

Pamela joined in the sentiment. 'Oh yes, it seems silly for a grown man to be calling me aunt. How old are you now, James?'

'Twenty-seven next up, err, Pamela.' Her name seemed to stick in his mouth and for a moment it was hard to get it out. She smiled, sensing his difficulty. 'You'll soon get used to it. Anthony is right, first names are best. Now what will you have to drink? There is a very good sherry or a madeira – unless, of course, you would prefer something else. I can offer you whisky or cognac?'

'Sherry sounds fine.'

'We have a couple of friends coming over for dinner,' the Brigadier announced, lifting his glass. Lady Pamela handed Astley his glass. He raised it. 'Cheerio, and here's to a jolly good Christmas.'

'Tallyho,' the Brigadier grinned. 'Have a seat, dear boy, make yerself at home.'

Astley settled into an armchair and stretched out his legs. 'Look forward to a spot of bittern watching tomorrow. The view from my room is dashed good.'

The Brigadier nodded. 'You need to be careful if you're going out on the marshes, dear boy. They can be treacherous if you don't know them. They've swallowed up more than one unwary victim, you know.'

'I'll remember to be careful.'

The Brigadier frowned and looked thoughtful. 'Tell you what, why don't I get old Morton Wolston to take you around.'

Astley sat up. 'Morton Wolston, is he still around. Blimey, he must be ancient by now.'

'Yes, he's still soldiering on, not full-time any more but he comes and does odd jobs for me around the grounds. Still cuts grass with a sickle – won't use a mower. He has a small dinghy – he could take you out and point you in the right direction. Don't know anyone who knows the reed beds better than Morton.'

'Right ho, that sounds useful.' Astley paused for a moment, a sudden image of the girl lying in the snow had slipped into his mind. 'That was a strange business with that child I knocked down as I arrived this evening. Shook me up a bit, I must say. The parents' reaction was jolly queer. Do you think I ought to go back in the morning and apologise? Just make sure the child is all right.'

The Brigadier looked momentarily concerned and his face darkened for a second or two – as if a cloud had just passed over his mind. 'No need to do that, James,' he said briskly. 'I'll pop along and see them in the morning. From what you've said it'll be the Fendyke's girl, Maisie. I know Ralph, he's the church sexton; it'll be better coming from me.' Astley was about to pursue it further and had just embarked on a suggestion that he ought to at least accompany him but the Brigadier cut it short and changed the subject.

'We've invited the Pearsons for supper. Bob's an old army chum of mine. They'll be over shortly. His wife Val's a bit of a mouse, but Bob's okay; I'm sure you'll get on hugely with him. Thought we'd all go out for a bit of a shoot on Boxing Day. Lots of good partridge around at the moment.'

The proposal put Astley in a bit of a quandary. He had come to the Hall with the intention of watching birds, not shooting them, but it was awkward; he didn't really want to upset his host. He decided the best course was to say nothing and shoot to miss on the day. He could always put it down to being a rotten shot. He was hunting around for something else to talk about when he was saved by the arrival of the Pearsons.

'Bob and I go back a long way,' the Brigadier gave his guest a hearty slap on the back. 'Knew him before he met Val here. Served together in the Transvaal wars under Buller. What a mess that was; poor old Buller was completely out of his depth. Total cock-up.' The two men rumbled off into a deep, raucous laugh.

Valerie Pearson and Lady Pamela excused themselves and went off in search of Mrs M and cook to take command of the dining arrangements.

'First time here, James?' Pearson asked during a pause in the military talk.

'No, but I haven't really been here in years, not since I was a child. We used to visit when my father and mother were alive. Both dead now, unfortunately.'

'Bad luck.'

'Motor accident. Father died on the spot, steering column went right through his chest, instantaneous. Mother survived for nearly two weeks then succumbed to septicaemia; blood poisoning.'

'Tragic to lose both. Were you very young at the time?'

'No, no, early twenties. It happened six years back.'

Bob Pearson was nodding sagely and Astley was looking for something to say when, for no better reason than it was on his mind, said, 'I was involved in a bit of an accident this evening as I arrived here. I knocked a small child over in the road. Couldn't help it, she just bolted out of nowhere. A family called Fendyke. Do you know of them?'

Pearson looked uncomfortable. He shot a glance over at the Brigadier. 'Have you told young James here about the history of this place? Dates back to the Black Prince, you know.' Astley nodded but in his mind it was clear that Pearson had wanted to avoid the subject of Maisie Fendyke and the accident.

'There's been a Boyes at Breydon ever since 1331,' the Brigadier cut in. 'The land was gifted by Edward the Third to my ancestor; reward for his part in bringing down the Earl of March, that usurper, Roger Mortimer. Ha!

Served the blighter right, he was a thoroughly bad lot that Mortimer chap.'

Dinner was to be a formal affair. It would start with game soup, then a roast of beef and a sherry trifle. It was to be followed by a ripe Stilton cheese, sticks of celery, nuts and a decanted bottle of port.

'Come on, I'll show you the cellar.' The Brigadier slapped a hand on Astley's shoulder. 'Follow me. We shall need a couple of bottles of claret for the beef, and something sweet for that pud – and a bottle of port for the Stilton.'

The cellar ran the length and half the breadth of the Hall. It had been carefully racked and labelled by the Brigadier's grandfather and held a good stock of fine old Napoleon brandy. By the light of an electric torch they found two good bottles of Chateaux Margaux claret. Further along the racks the Brigadier plucked a half bottle of Tokay and held it up to examine the colour.

'Only good thing to come out of Hungary,' he grunted, then laughed. He handed the bottle to Astley. 'Port,' he shouted with enthusiasm and marched on along the rows of bottles. He stopped abruptly and Astley nearly fell over him.

'1904, just the job.' The Brigadier removed a bottle from where it rested, cradled in the rack. He passed it gently to Astley, keeping it horizontal. 'Keep it flat and don't shake it or it won't be drinkable for a week. We'll get Parky to decant it; he's the expert in these things.'

As they made their way back towards the cellar steps Astley again broached the subject of the accident. 'I've been thinking about little Maisie Fendyke …'.

The Brigadier cut him short. 'Well don't,' he said in a voice that had the ring of sombre disapproval. 'It's better you leave that to me.'

They climbed up the steps in an awkward silence but when they reached the top the Brigadier's mood lightened. 'Come on. We'll give these to Parky and then I suggest we get another drink down us. Oh, by the way, did I mention, our local vicar will be joining us for the festive feast on Christmas day?'

They sat him between Valerie Pearson and Lady Pamela, which quite suited him as he had little in common with the two men whose conversation largely circulated around old campaigns and whether this new disability they were calling 'shell shock' was nothing more than a lack of moral fibre. When he did interject briefly into the conversation with what he considered a reasonable explanation of battle trauma the other two looked at him appalled and he backed away.

Valerie Pearson sensed the awkward moment and came to his rescue. 'James, do tell me about this bird watching that you do, it sounds awfully interesting. You've come to study our bitterns, Bob tells me.'

Astley grasped at the opportunity. 'Yes, the brown heron. It's quite a rare species. Its habitat is marshlands. It inhabits the reed beds of the southeast, so not a lot of places to study it. The Fens are one of the best places in the country to find them.'

'Do you intend to write about them?' Lady Pamela asked politely, but with an air that betrayed a slight indifference. 'A treatise – or a slim volume perhaps?'

Astley shook his head. 'Not really. I'm hoping for some photographs; it's just a hobby really. I belong to a society in London. We organise weekends in the country, that sort of thing.'

'How interesting,' Lady Pamela paused while she gave some attention to what was on the plate in front of her. It briefly crossed Astley's mind that these two women did not find his passion in the least interesting and he was pleased when Valerie Pearson changed the subject.

'What do you do in London?' she asked politely.

'I work for the National Provincial Bank. I'm an undermanager in the Holborn branch.'

She had begun to say, 'How interesting ...' but was cut short. The door from the kitchen opened. The housekeeper, Mrs M, stood there for a moment; she gave a short bow-come-nod in the direction of Lady Pamela.

'Excuse me, ma'am.' Her face was taught and there was a look of what Astley thought was mild fear in the widened eyes that briefly darted around the table. She stepped quickly over to the Brigadier and spoke softly in a tone that was inaudible. The Brigadier's face took on a look of anger.

'Bob, give me a hand.' The two men got up hastily from their chairs, briefly acknowledged the ladies and left the room.

For a moment Astley said nothing; he just sat looking from one woman to the other with a mild expression of questioning on his face. Then Lady Pamela stood up and excused herself. As she opened the door to leave the room he thought he heard something like the cry of a woman's voice coming from somewhere in the house. Valerie Pearson picked up her wine glass and sipped at its contents.

'Nothing to worry about,' she said, creasing her face with what Astley thought was a forced smile. 'Poachers, James; it'll be the partridge they're after – that or the pheasants. Anthony gets very upset about them.'

From outside there was the muffled sound of a shotgun report followed by two more. Valerie Pearson feigned to ignore the sound, then under the cover of a little nervous laugh said, 'I'm sure the boys will handle it.'

It was no more than ten minutes before everyone returned. The Brigadier and Bob Pearson were the first to come back.

'Poachers,' she immediately exclaimed. 'I was telling James here that they are such a nuisance at this time of the year.'

The Brigadier nodded. 'Poachers, quite so.' He sat down heavily in his chair. 'Poachers, damn nuisance.' Bob Pearson was nodding vigorous agreement when Lady Pamela came back in. Both men looked at her; she gave the slightest upward nod with the trace of a smile.

'All's well,' she said. 'Now who's for trifle? Anthony, dear, get Parkinson to pour the Tokay.' The mood lightened and the conversation reverted back to normality.

'Do you often get poachers around here?' Astley raised his glass, 'In which case here's good riddance to them.' The others laughed and raised their own glasses to return the toast.

That night as he got undressed and into his pyjamas he found himself humming the tune he had heard when he was out by the car in the snow. It had a familiar ring to it – but he couldn't place it.

CHAPTER 3

The brown heron

The morning was bright and he woke to a shaft of pure snowlight, edged with the gold of a rising sun, piercing the gap in the curtains. He pulled on a wool dressing gown and went over to the radiator, pressing the back of his legs against it and enjoying the warmth. He had slept solidly and felt ready for the day. Moving to the window he drew back the heavy drapes and allowed the light to flood in; there he stood for a moment in the bay, enjoying the scene, gazing out across the expanse of Breydon Water to the snow covered reed beds on the far side – and farther, on to a lonely windmill perched on the horizon. Collecting his binoculars from the dressing table he trained them on the marshes, scanning the opposite side of the river. He did not really expect to see anything but as he took the glasses away from his eyes he caught sight of a dark object coming out of the distance. Quickly he brought up the binoculars again and trained them on what was clearly a bird. At first he took it to be a Canada goose. It was about the right size and they were in the area, overwintering away from the deep freeze of the North American winter. Half a minute later it turned and he saw the profile; it was a bittern, his first sighting and he could hardly contain his excitement. He followed it with the glasses as the bird turned and made a graceful descent into the marshes almost opposite the house on the far bank of the river. That did it, he would go out straight away after breakfast and do a reccy of the area.

Over a breakfast of crisp bacon and scrambled eggs he discussed his plans for the day.

'Are you a collector?' Lady Pamela asked, 'Do you have a birds' egg collection?'

'Well, sort of I suppose; but it's not a real collection, it's photographs – I'm compiling a work; a handbook on some of the rarer birds in the country – and, of course, there are pictures of the eggs.'

Lady Pamela smiled. 'Do let me refresh your teacup.' She swirled the pot and concluding that she was not happy with its contents called Parker. 'Ask Mrs M to make me a fresh pot, will you. Now, where were we, oh yes, that sounds very exciting – do you have a publisher in mind.'

Ashley shook his head. 'Not really, it's early days yet. I think I'll go for a reccy after breakfast, just get the lay of the land.'

Overnight the snow cover had taken a frost and now there was a slight crunch underfoot. He stepped out from the cover of the porch and stood for a moment surveying the scene. He looked to where his car was parked; half the snow had been melted by the heat of the engine and it had slithered off the bonnet forming small frozen mounds by the front wheels. His eye was drawn to an irregular shadow on the driver's door panel. He went over to it and rubbed his hand across a shallow dent. It must have been where the child had hit it. That was such a close call and it still worried his conscience that he had not been back to visit the parents to make sure the child was fit and well.

As he walked ankle-deep down the drive which led to the lane beyond he picked up the footprints of Bob Pearson and the Brigadier. He followed them to where they stopped at the edge of a thick belt of reeds that covered the bank of the river as it made its final hundred yards to flow into the great pool that was Breydon Water. Somewhere in those reeds, or those on the other side, he hoped to find his bittern. There would be no nests and, of course, no eggs, but the bird would be spotted more easily against the snowy landscape and he hoped to get a few decent pictures. A glint of gold light caught his eye and, looking closer, he saw the bright red of a discarded shotgun cartridge. It lay there in the snow like a bright jewel, fresh and free from snow. He stooped and retrieved it, holding the open end to his nose. It had the sulphuric smell of burnt powder. Then he saw another lying a short distance from where he had spotted the first. It must, he concluded, have been the shots he'd heard when the Brigadier and Bob Pearson had gone after the poachers. He carelessly discarded the empty shells and began walking in the direction of Breydon Water.

The foray had not produced a bittern sighting but he was not surprised; he would need to get across the river and into the expanse of marshes that lay on the far side. All he had encountered was a flock of reed buntings, a handful of coots and some moorhens, the latter's distinctive red flash making them stand out against the snowy background. An hour later he returned to the house. At the front of the building he stopped to admire the sweep of the roofline with its tall barley sugar chimneys and an iron weathervane perched on a turret that must have originally served as a defensive lookout. It was then that he became aware of a face looking down at him from a dormer window just next to the turret. It was the face of a girl. He waved but whoever it was must have stepped back from the window because the next minute she had gone. He lingered for a moment but the girl did not reappear so he carried on, going round to the back of the house where he would go in through the kitchen and avoid bringing his snow-caked boots into the front lobby. He stamped them hard on the flagstones outside the back door, knocking off the snow then rubbing the soles clean on an iron foot-scraper.

'Good morning, Master James.'

Astley looked round. A short man wearing stout leather gaiters that ran from his ankles to his knee stood there grinning. He had on a heavy woollen overcoat, half open at the front to display a moleskin jacket, a black waistcoat and a white shirt, the separate collar of which had been detached. He was an elderly man with thick grey hair and a bushy moustache, but he still held himself straight and his chest stood out like a barrel.

'By Jove, it's Morton, isn't it? Well, I never; I haven't seen you since I was ten.'

'Well, now,' Morton said in his sing-song Norfolk accent and handed over a bundle of freshly cut mistletoe. 'You'd best take this if you be goin' inside, Master James. Save my ol' boots maken a mess'av Mrs M's kitchen.'

The thought of a ride out to the marshes came into his mind and he decided he would take the opportunity to broach the subject. 'The Brigadier tells me you have a boat and you might be persuaded to take me over onto the reed beds, Morton.'

'O aye, Master James – and when'd you be wantin' a go then?'

'This afternoon perhaps, straight after lunch.'

Morton Wolston shuffled a bit. 'Well, now, if you come doon ter the slipway at one o'clock she'll be in the water. We shan't have long y'understand; sun goes down at four, Master James.' He shook his head sagely. 'Wouldn't do to be caught out there on them reeds in the dark now.'

The Swallow was a ten-foot clinker-built dinghy with a small paraffin outboard motor. Morton pushed it off into the flow of the ebbing river, letting it drift towards the estuary and Breydon Water. He stood up in the stern, his short, stocky figure bent over the outboard as he wound a cord round its flywheel. He gave the cord a hard tug, spinning the flywheel; the engine puttered but failed to start. He wound and pulled again. The little dinghy rocked wildly from side to side under the inertia of Morton's activity. He turned to Astley with a broad smile as the boat got caught up in the gathering pace of the tide and headed out into open water. 'Now then, Master James, you put them ro'locks in and get those oars working, else we'll be in Yarmouth afore ya know it.'

   Astley fumbled the rowlocks into their holes, pinned them in place and dropped the oars into their upturned cups. He started to row against the tide while Morton carried on pulling on the whipcord, every pull rocking the boat alarmingly so that they almost shipped water.

Rowing in short, hard strokes Astley managed to hold the dinghy against the tide but not much more than that. Unless Morton could get the outboard going they would have little hope of getting back upstream to the slipway again, and he began to have images of sitting out in the slough of Breydon's expanse until slack water, which could be several hours away. That was when it dawned on him that the wool coat he was wearing might not be enough protection, especially if a wind got up.

As his hopes began to slump there was a popping, spluttering noise and the outboard motor sprang into life. Morton sat down heavily, causing the dinghy to lurch again. 'Ship they oars, Master James,' he sang out.

The little engine got the better of the tide and they started to beat their way back upstream away from Breydon and over to the far shore. 'Oi'll get thee up above the slip, then we'll be havin' the toid with us, Master.'

As the dinghy bumped against the caked mud of the bank Morton leaned out and grabbed a handful of the long reeds. Again the dinghy leaned precariously as he pulled them close in to the shore. Astley flinched for fear that he would upset the small craft and tip them both into the icy water, but Morton seemed unconcerned. From the bottom of the dinghy he picked up a long metal mooring hook with a rope attached, and with a single swing drove it deep into the roots of the reeds. He tied off one end to the stern of *The Swallow* and then, in an action that was extraordinary for a man of his age, nimbly hopped ashore. Standing with his feet on two clumps of reeds he lifted a boot and, using the heel, rammed the mooring spike down into the reed bed where it would stay until he pulled it out.

'Now you throw that painter here, Master James,' he called, pointing to a rope attached to the bow of the dinghy. Astley threw the line ashore and, catching it in one hand, Morton tied it off to a thick bunch of reeds, which he then knotted around the rope. Holding the dinghy close to shore he put out a hand and took a firm hold of Astley's arm and hauled him out.

He was no sooner ashore than he realised this was not the way to do things. The reeds were tall, in some places as high as his chest and never less than waist high. Movement was difficult.

'Now mind your step on they roots, Master James, I don't want you go sinking down into that there mud 'cos you won't as not get oot that easy.'

The best Astley could manage was to blunder along in the footsteps of Morton and shortly after they set out he decided to call a halt to the expedition. He looked through the gaps in the tall stems of the plants as they bent and swayed to a gathering breeze. Here and there he caught sight of the brown plush heads of bulrushes that had infiltrated and taken root among the more common reeds. Then for an instance he thought he caught sight of a brighter colour floating in the sea of waving green.

'What's that?' he called to Morton and pointed to something bright blue that seemed to be clinging to the head of a bulrush. Astley squelched his way to where the thing twitched and rippled in the moving air. As he plucked it free he saw it was nothing more than a scrap of hair ribbon. He turned to retrace his steps and his eye fell on another object. He bent down and picked it from the muddy pool in which it lay. It was a child's shoe.

'What do you make of that?' He held up the shoe and the ribbon. Morton said nothing for a moment, then shrugged off the question. 'Most loik that'll have bin brought up on the toid. All manner o' things comes up with the water.'

They made their way back to where *The Swallow* had been left and with the outboard's exhaust puttering out over the now ebbing water they made their way back to the slipway. He thanked Morton for his assistance but the old man would hear nothing of it. It was, he insisted, a pleasure to help both Astley and the Brigadier. 'You know, Master James,' he said, stopping and turning to look back at the horizon, 'if you want to get a good view over these marshes then you could do worse than go out to Handley's old mill.' He pointed out to the black-and-white mill that Astley had seen from his bedroom window.

'My son, George, he knows them Handleys. He could like as not get you the key.'

At the bottom of the lane leading to the Hall Morton took his leave and started to walk towards the village, a solitary silhouette in the failing light of the afternoon. The low sun threw a long shadow off the disappearing figure and soon there was nothing but the track of his footprints traced out in the snow. Astley reached the house and, looking up, noticed there was a light in the window where he had seen the face of the girl. He wondered who she was and it crossed his mind to ask the Brigadier over supper.

Up in his room he shrugged off his overcoat and hung it in the wardrobe. He removed the little shoe that he had stuffed into his pocket together with the blue ribbon. At first, when he had caught a glimpse of the ribbon, he had thought it might be a kingfisher. He laid them both on the top of the chest of drawers then he smiled to himself at the sum of the afternoon's work.

The brown heron had eluded him and instead he had these strange mementoes of … of what? He tried to think for a moment of who might have been the owner – and how they came to lose one shoe in the marshes. Maybe Morton was right, maybe they did come in on the tide.

CHAPTER 4

The village

The walk to the village was bracing and just what he had needed. He had eaten too well and drunk too much at supper the night before; he was not used to such a rich spread and the chance to walk it off was welcomed. The snow lay still largely undisturbed and he could see clearly the distinctive prints of Morton's hob-nailed boots.

Entering into the square the footprints merged with others until the ground became an undecipherable turmoil of churned-up grey. He made his way past the war memorial, crossing over to the Breydon Arms public house where he pushed open the door to the Public Bar. Inside, the air was warm and smoky; men were leaning against the counter, pints of ale to hand, or sitting at tables playing dominoes and cribbage. At the far end of the room a log fire was burning in an open hearth, the brilliant ruby embers snapping and crackling, sending hot showers of sparks flurrying upwards.

'What'll it be now, sir?' The barman gave him a cheerful grin.

'I'll have a pint of bitter, thank you. I'm looking for George Wolston; I've been told I might find him here.' The barman pulled a glass from the shelf behind him and, pulling down hard on the beer pump, sent a gush of pale gold liquid sloshing into it.

'George Wolston,' he shouted across the bar towards the fire, as he continued to pump out the beer. 'Summen 'ere ta see you.' A youngish man detached himself from a small huddle that was standing around the fire and came over to where Astley stood.

'Arter noon, sir. You'll be Master James, oim gessen.' He gave a little tug on the peak of his cloth cap.

'Your father told me you had a key to Handley's mill and I was wondering if I could persuade you to take me there.'

George Wolston pulled a pocket watch out of his waistcoat and opened the case. 'Oi don't rightly think I can, sir. Oi 'ave ter be away ter Yarm'uth – but you tak this; you can let yerself in.' He pulled a large, ancient iron key out of one of the patch pockets on his coat. 'You ha ter moind them stairs, though; they'm not be what they were. Rot got in em.'

Astley took the giant key and looked at it for a moment. 'Are you sure Mr Handley won't mind? Me being a stranger and all that.'

George gave a slight sideways nod of his head. 'You don't worry on that account, sir. Old Handley ees gone. Ee died this Christmas a year back. Only old missus and er is past carin. No, you just let yerself in; ha a moind about them steps though, sir. You can come to the mill fust turn off the Acle Road. Just you folla the dyke – you can't miss it. It stand up there loik a big ol tree.'

Out in the street again he stopped momentarily to take in the scene. It was, he thought, the image of a traditional Christmas card: the church covered in snow, the pub alive with light and music, there was even a robin perched on the folded hands of the soldier on the war memorial. The only thing missing was a snowman. Then it struck him: there were no children; it was a Christmas scene with no children. Shame, he said to himself and started back in the direction of the Hall where he would collect the Lagonda and go over to Handley's mill. As he trod down the snow another thing struck him: all the footprints were adults. He stopped and looked at the track coming and going into the village square; there were no traces of children's feet. When he thought about it he had not seen a child, other than Maisie Fendyke, since he had arrived. Then his mind went to the face in the window back at the Hall, the girl who had been looking down at him, but she was older. He would have expected to see the smaller children out playing in the snow, building snowmen, throwing snowballs – but there were none. How very odd, he mused, a village without children. No, that can't be right. Perhaps they were in school; that must be it.

When he got to the Hall he found Morton clearing away the snow from the driveway; he had also cleaned it off Astley's car. 'That be a nice motor Master James.' He looked admiringly at the car. He took out a pipe already charged with black tobacco, struck a match and drew hard on it, then blew the smoke out in a great cloud of blue-grey smoke.

'Lagonda,' Astley said proudly, 'two litre. Thanks for cleaning the snow off it, Morton.'

Morton gave him a homely smile. 'No need for the thanks, Master James, just doin' the job.' Astley looked slightly embarrassed but then a thought occurred to him.

'Morton, I've just been to the village and I find it curious. There weren't any children out playing. Is that usual?'

Morton was silent for a minute, as if the question was unwelcome. 'Mothers probably don't want them gettin' cold,' he finally offered.

'Well I've never heard of that before. Are they still in school?'

Morton seemed uncomfortable. 'Can't rightly say.' He half muttered the words under his breath then quickly added, 'Excuse me, Master James, but oi have ta get on.'

'Of course,' Astley said politely, then got into the car and started the engine. He let it run for a while just ticking over to warm the engine. After a few minutes he turned on the heater fan and waited for the mist to clear from the windscreen.

On the road back into the village he passed the house of Ralph Fendyke and, seeing him in the cottage clearing snow, stopped and got out. As he approached Fendyke put down the shovel and held up his hand to shade his eyes so that he could see who was coming his way.

As Astley walked through the gate a woman appeared at the front door. She was small, with a time-worn face and she held herself in a rounded stoop, as if she carried the care of her family heavily about her shoulders; he supposed her to be the mother.

'Good morning,' Astley called to them.

Fendyke took off his cap and held it down by his side. 'Good morning, sir, how can I help ee?'

'I'm James Astley. It was my car that unfortunately knocked your little girl down the other evening. I just felt I ought to come and say how sorry I was and ask if she is all right.'

Fendyke turned to the woman. 'This be moi woif, sir, Alice, an' God bless you, sir, but the littl'un be just foin.'

'Yes, God bless ee, sir,' the woman half whispered, 'she be roit as rain.'

'Well, I am most sorry and beg your pardon.'

The woman looked nervous and Fendyke cut in across her. 'You don't need to be a sayin that, sir.'

'No, no,' the woman insisted, but as she protested with increasing urgency the diminutive figure of Maisie appeared behind her, clutching at her mother's dress, peering diffidently at the stranger at their door. 'She's always running off, sir; we ha ta keep her indoors; twasn't your fault she ran inta your motor car. Oi ope it did no damage, sir.'

Astley was about to assure her that the car was fine when he noticed something not quite right. The girl was wearing odd shoes. He stared at her feet for a moment.

'Did your little girl lose a shoe on the marshes?' He looked from one to the other of the parents. They both stared blankly back at him, their eyes furtive and, he thought, there was a hint of fear buried deep inside them.

The look on their faces did not seem right; it was strained, as if they had been confronted by their own guilt in some illicit enterprise. It left him puzzled and ill at ease. He had wanted only to reassure them of his contrition over the matter but instead seemed to have put them into some inexplicable fear.

'Only I found one identical to that,' he continued, now slightly bemused, 'on the other side of the river – in the reed bed. How on earth did it get over there?'

Fendyke furrowed his brow and rubbed the stubble on his chin. 'Most loikly it got taken there by some animal. There's otters a plenty in these parts. Maybe one of them bitte'ns carried it away, sir.'

'Strange,' Astley smiled and half laughed. 'OK. Well, if there's nothing I can do I'll at least bring the shoe back.'

The woman again looked troubled. She put an arm around Maisie, holding her tight, as if she were afraid the child might bolt. 'Oh, you should'na be a worrying with that, sir, really now.'

'Least I can do.' Sensing there was nothing more he could say Astley left them and, getting into the Lagonda, headed out of the village towards Great Yarmouth and the Acle Road.

Handley's mill stood out on the horizon, a round black stump of a building heaving up from the flat landscape, its sails feathered and locked so they would not stir even in the strongest gale. Its top was capped with a white painted hood which looked like a Dutch bonnet. As he got closer he could see a trellis of wooden steps climbing up the side of the mill; they rose in one single rickety flight to where they terminated at a door that was let into the curved flank of the building.

He parked the car and got out, standing for a moment looking away across the marshland that was now surrounding him. There was a slight breeze, nothing much, barely enough just to ripple the surface of the reeds as it blew in a whisper across them. Above, the sky was a clear, icy blue and with the still rising sun behind him the conditions for his observations were close to perfect. Morton had been right; the mill would make a perfect hide.

From the back seat of the Lagonda he took out a wicker case then, with a pair of binoculars hung around his neck, put one foot on the first tread of the stairs and began the climb. When he reached the top he stopped for a brief moment and looked into the distance to where Breydon Water spread itself out into the various channels that criss-crossed the marshes; channels hacked out by the reed-cutters who culled the stems to make thatch. The exposed banks of the channels, normally coated with black mud, were now a pristine white from their covering of snow. It could not be better. The brown form of the bittern would display in perfect contrast with the banks on which it would come to stand, motionless in its patient vigil, its pin-sharp eyes piercing the water as it waited to stab its lunch.

The iron key ground in the lock; there was a 'clack' as the bolt drew back, then a groan as the weight of the opening door bore down on the hinges; they were in need of grease. Inside it was dark and the air smelled of damp. In the middle of the room in which he stood he could just make out the main shaft descending from the headgear high above. It extended through the ceiling to the floor where it located into a housing with a huge toothed flywheel and transfer gears that drove the pump in the housing at the base. The mill's function was to drain the water from the adjacent land, keeping the pastures from flooding.

He left the door open, letting in enough light to search for the paraffin lamps that George Wolston had told him were stored in a cupboard, together with a drum of paraffin oil. As he stumbled his way in the gloom he heard the rustling sound of disturbed vermin; there were rats.

With a lamp lit, he pulled shut the door and locked it. Then he started to climb the roughhewn wooden stairway that spiralled up to the floor above. The stairs were not good; the mill was more than fifty years old and the damp salt air had taken its toll on the iron nails that held the treads in place – rusting them away to a crumbling oxide. He climbed with caution, testing each step with the pressure of his foot before placing his full weight onto it.

Reaching the next level, he found what he was looking for, a door that let out onto a balcony that girdled the mill. This would be his observation platform. He opened the wicker case and removed a small folding stool with a canvas seat; he set it down on the balcony. Using a wooden box that he had found in the mill, he placed it alongside the stool to use as a table. From the basket he took out a paper package containing some sandwiches together with a thermos flask of tea. He moved to the edge of the balcony and, holding his binoculars up to his eyes, slowly panned along the first of the reed cutter's dykes. The dykes had been hewn in straight lines with right-angled intersections that made the marshland look like some kind of giant children's game with the squares of dark reeds bordered in white, a sort of hop-scotch.

It was not long before he caught sight of the first bittern. It stood rigidly on one of the banks, its neck stretched towards the water, its knife-sharp bill ready to strike at the smelt and the eels that swam in the dykes. The bird presented a perfect profile, stark against the whiteness of its surroundings. Astley let the binoculars drop and hang round his neck. He went into the shoulder bag he had been carrying and took out a camera. From a small leather pouch in the bag he removed a telescopic lens: German – a precision military instrument of high quality. His father had brought it home from the Great War, a trophy captured together with a Leica camera.

He had shot several frames when the bird suddenly took fright and launched itself lightly into the air. As it flapped away across the horizon he attempted to follow it with the lens but the field of vision was too narrow and in the end he put down the camera. Seating himself on the canvas stool, he unscrewed the top of the thermos flask and poured out a stream of steaming tea into a cup. He took a sandwich from the paper bag and settled down to eat his lunch.

It was gone two o'clock and the quality of the light would not last much longer. He had drained the dregs of his tea cup and was preparing to pick up the binoculars again when his attention was caught by the sound of singing. It appeared to come from below the mill, possibly inside and his first thought was that someone had entered the building, but he was sure he had locked the door. Out of curiosity he stood up and leaned over the balcony rail but there was nothing. The strains of the tune that wafted up to him were familiar; after a few moments he recognised it as the one he had heard on the evening he had knocked down Maisie Fendyke. It had the lilt of a nursery rhyme about it. Stepping back inside the body of the mill, he turned up the wick on the paraffin lamp and, holding it up in front of him, made his way to the head of the stairs.

The voice of a woman seemed to be coming from the floor below. On the first step he paused, trying to catch the words of the song; he got the refrain but then the voice stopped and there was nothing but silence, punctuated only by the creak of the tread under the pressure of his foot. He waited a little longer then continued on down the stairs. Just before he reached the last turn in the spiral the strains of the tune drifted up again. A vague childhood memory sprung into his mind as he recognised the tune; of course, it was the ancient nursery rhyme 'Boys and Girls Come Out to Play' ... but the words that came were different. He stood listening, fascinated by the pure quality of the voice that was singing and the words he now caught ...

Following, following always to roam;
Following, following leaving your home.
Follow the music that leads you away;
Hoping you'll come back one happy day.

Climb up the stairs and into your bed;
Pull up the blanket and over your head.
Don't hark to the music or you will be led
To the place where you'll be until you be dead.

Following, following, list'ning too long;
Following, following, things do go wrong ...

The voice stopped again and there was silence. He waited but nothing more came. Descending carefully down the last few steps he reached the floor and the room came into view. As he held up the lamp he saw there was a woman there. She was standing with her back to him, facing the wall and the first thought was that it must be Mrs Handley come to see who was in her mill. But the figure was that of a young woman, slim with flaxen shoulder length hair. She seemed not to be aware of him and again broke into the song. He wasn't sure what to do and for a moment he felt like an intruder, someone who should not be there. He cleared his throat because he could not think of what to say but he needed to announce his presence. Slowly the woman turned and in that moment he saw what he took to be a great sadness in her eyes. For an instant she seemed to look right through him. She screamed a piercing, shrieking scream that hit him full in the face and sent a cold shiver through him. What happened next was too quick to relate. She fled across the room and disappeared down the final flight of stairs to the floor below. Astley stood frozen, rooted to the spot, horrified by the events that had just transpired.

Pulling himself back to reality, he made his way cautiously down to the room below. The woman was nowhere to be seen; she had vanished. She must, he concluded, have left through the door that led to the outside staircase. He walked over to it, still slightly shaken. The door was locked, exactly as he had left it. He turned and, holding up the lamp above his head, walked the full circle of the room. There was no one, the mill was empty. He stood in disbelief. How could this be? As he applied his mind to the conundrum, his sense of pragmatism took over and he concluded the only logical explanation: the woman had a key. Slowly a smile crept onto his face; from the scream she had uttered and the way she had fled he supposed she must have thought him a spectre of the old mill owner, Handley.

Climbing back up to the top floor he hung the lamp on a beam and went out onto the balcony. The incident, which had shaken him to start with, was now receding to the back of his mind and he once more picked up the binoculars and scanned the reed beds hoping to find another bittern. Instead, he saw a figure in the distance over towards Breydon Water where one of the rivers ran into it. He adjusted the focus and as he did he recognised the woman he'd disturbed in the mill. How curious that she should be standing out there, seemingly just gazing out across the waters;

and even more curious that she had managed to pick her way across the reed beds in that short space of time. He concluded she must be with the reed cutters and familiar with the marshes. He picked up the camera and trained the telescopic lens on the woman. It was stronger than the binoculars and the image it gave him was much clearer. As he watched her, the woman turned towards him and looked hard in his direction – it was as if she could see him watching her; but at that distance without the advantage of binoculars or a telescope, how could she? Without thinking he pressed the shutter release and took her photo. Almost as a reflex action he repeated the operation – twice. It was as if there was a fascination he could not resist.

The evening set in and the light faded. He packed the stool and the thermos into the case, put the camera and lens into the shoulder bag, and made his way down through the mill to the door. Hearing the key snatch open the lock and the door groan on its hinges a thought struck him and he realised he had not heard these sounds when the woman had entered the mill; then again, he rationalised, he was out on the balcony so he probably would not have heard it. But how had she managed to leave so quickly and so silently. He had been in the room above when she fled, surely he would have heard the grinding of the rusty door hinges.

He locked the mill door and climbed down the outer steps. By the time he reached the Lagonda it was dark. He stowed his bag and case in the back, wound the engine into life and turned on the headlights. The lane that had led him to the mill was little more than a track and in the dark the edges were indistinct and difficult to see; a wrong move and he realised he could end up rolling off the edge and into the dyke that ran alongside it. If that happened the car would sink into the deep mud of the marsh and he would probably be sucked under with it.

He slowed to not much more than a fast walking pace, wound down the window and stuck his head out to get a better view of where the edge of the track lay. He was close to reaching the main road and could see the lights on the outskirts of Great Yarmouth when he saw the woman again. Quite without warning she was there on the far side of the dyke, standing in the reeds just looking at him. The shock of seeing her took his concentration off the road and in those seconds he felt the front wheel leave the track and slide towards the dyke.

'My God!' he blurted out loud, 'she's going over.'

In a reflex of adrenalin he wrestled with the steering as the weight of the Lagonda began to drag the car deeper into the soft snow-covered ground of the embankment. Then the back end began to slew closer to the water's edge. In a moment of horror he realised the game was up and he had little hope of saving it. He began shouting at the car in wild and crazed encouragement, 'Come on girl,' he yelled at it, 'you can do it – get your arse out of the water you daft cow. Come on, come on, come on.'

He felt the car lean and he knew it was going over. If it rolled into the dyke he was a dead man, for sure. He would never get out from under that heavy chassis – he would be crushed, smothered and choked in the thick black mud. He saw the woman's face, like a flash of white in the headlights and in that split second he thought it must be a death hallucination and that he was already gone.

There was a bone-shaking thump and a bang; the tail end of the Lagonda felt as if it had been kicked upwards and it shot sideways in a mad leap. The back wheels were up on the track again, gripping and showering up stones and shingle. Manically he hauled on the steering wheel, wrenching the front of the car away from the waters of the dyke. For a few more yards the front wheels resisted, caught by the muddy snow and refusing to lift out of it. Then with a lurch the whole car was back on the track. He had made it.

Sweating and trembling, he pulled the machine to a halt and got out. He looked back into the dark to where he had almost come to grief. There was no sign of the woman. Slowly his composure returned. 'Bloody hell,' he said under his breath, 'that was a close one.'

He made no mention of the incident when he got back to the Hall and he remained silent about the woman he had encountered in the mill. It somehow seemed too fanciful and he thought it best kept to himself.

That night in his room as he got ready for bed he found himself humming; it was the tune the woman had sung and the words of rhyme were going round in his head.

CHAPTER 5

The woman in the marsh

His head was barely on the pillow when he heard the sound of running. Someone had come up the stairs in a hurry. There were voices, urgent and muffled; the sound of panic and the headlong flight of feet rushing to the upper floor. There was a moment of quiet, then the sound of people out on the drive. The front door banged shut and the strains of urgent voices reached him. He got out of bed and went to the bay window, pulling back the drapes to get a view of what was going on. A bright silver moon reflected off the snow lighting up the faces of those assembled at the front of the house.

He could clearly make out the figures of the Brigadier and Ralph Fendyke. They looked agitated, especially Ralph Fendyke. Then a man he thought to be the vicar arrived. There was the air of a posse about them, a group of vigilantes, men bent on a mission of some urgency. As they hurried away in the direction of Breydon Water they were joined by others; he recognised the short robust figure of Morton Wolston. In the same moment he also noticed that everyone was armed; even the vicar carried a shotgun. The thought ran through his head that the poachers were back. He looked at his watch lying on the table by his bed; it was gone midnight. He was not sure what to make of it and for a while he just stood looking out at the now empty driveway below.

Two things caught his attention. The sound of a girl's voice, which seemed to be protesting, was coming from the floor above. There was the muffled sound of banging as if someone was pounding with their fists on a door. Astley moved to the door of his bedroom and opened it. It was a girl's voice, half screaming, half sobbing, and punctuated with the most mournful howls. He hurriedly pulled on his dressing gown and was halfway into the hall when another sound grabbed his attention – the sound of gunshots; not just a single shot or even one or two. There must have been twenty or more fired in rapid succession like a fusillade. Then, without warning, everything went quiet. It took a moment for it to sink in – the girl was no longer screaming, the thumping of fists on the door had stopped, the guns had gone silent. There was a detectable sibilance to the air, as if his ears had been shattered by an explosion of noise and were left whistling. Then he heard footsteps descending the stairs from the upper floor. He stepped out into the corridor and went quickly to the landing where he came face to face with Parkinson.

'What on earth was all that about, Parky?'

Parkinson shook his head, barely breaking his progress. 'Nothing to concern yourself about, Mr Astley. I should go back to bed if I were you. Good night, sir.' Parkinson moved on down the stairs leaving Astley standing there in a state of confusion.

Shortly after he had returned to his bedroom he heard the others coming back. There was the low grumble of voices, the sound of people in sombre conversation. Eventually he heard the front door close and shortly after that the house fell silent. For some time he lay in bed half listening out for sounds, though he had no idea what those would be. It had been an altogether strange day and an even stranger evening. In his mind he kept raking over the events: the screams and howls of the girl upstairs still echoed in his ears. It occurred to him that perhaps he should go up to the top of the house and try to locate the room where she was. But then what? He imagined from what he had heard that she must be locked in. Was she a prisoner? He shook the idea away – the Brigadier would never be party to such a thing. Maybe she was demented, mentally deficient and being kept locked away for her own good. He had heard of such things and that seemed the most plausible explanation. Then again, there was the business of the gunshots. It sounded like a pitched battle. Surely they could not have been firing at a poacher; the poor devil would have been ripped to shreds with all that lead shot. In the end he let it go and drifted off into sleep.

He went down to breakfast early with the intention of spending the morning developing his film.

'How do you propose to do that?' the Brigadier asked as he spread a thick layer of marmalade onto a piece of toast. 'Don't you need equipment and chemicals and that sort of stuff?'

'Indeed,' Astley agreed, 'but not that much. I thought I'd go into the village. I see you've got a chemist shop there. All I need is some hypo and developer. I have a developing drum and if Mrs M could find me a couple of shallow trays that's about it. I could use the laundry as a dark room; just hang up a couple of sheets at the windows to keep the light out – that should do it.'

The Brigadier grinned and bit heartily into his toast. 'Resourceful,' he spluttered through a mouth full of munched up bread and marmalade, 'that's what we like to see.' Lady Pamela looked at her husband in mild disapproval.

'Anthony, a man who talks with food in his mouth is in danger of betraying his upbringing.' Then she smiled to show that it was only a very minor admonishment and should be taken in good part.

Astley waited until they had finished breakfast and when he thought the moment was right said, 'I couldn't help hearing that bit of a ruckus going on last night; all those guns going off. What was that about?'

Lady Pamela looked sideways at her husband and then back at Astley. 'I must get on. I have to let Mrs M and cook know how many for Christmas dinner. You will excuse me, won't you?' Astley started to get up out of courtesy but she put out a hand. 'No, no, stay there, James. There's no need for you to rush.' The Brigadier ignored the question, taking the opportunity of his wife's interruption to sidestep it. Astley sensed the enquiry had been unwelcome but he was curious and pressed it.

'I hope you didn't mind me asking, but it seemed an unusual sort of occurrence.' The Brigadier's expression hardened.

'Just some local business,' he said, brushing it aside. 'Nothing for you to worry about.' He stood up. 'Well, must get on. Lots to do, being Christmas Eve tomorrow and all that, don't cha know. You carry on with your photographics, dear boy. Take yourself off to the chemist shop.' With that he left.

The walk to the chemist's shop took him past the village school. Inside there was a light showing and it occurred to him to look in and enquire about the children – or rather the absence of children.

He tried the latch on the door. It lifted easily – it was not locked. He pushed it open and stepped into the lobby. Through the glass of the next door, which led into the classroom, he could see the desks and chairs where the pupils sat, but there was no evidence of children. There was, however, a woman – a young woman, wearing spectacles with her fair hair rolled up into a bun. She was seated at a table placed at the head of the class and was occupied sorting through a pile of books. Astley tapped on the glass. The woman looked up and peered at him over the top of her spectacles. Seeing her smile he pushed the door open and entered. The young woman stood up in anticipation, waiting to see what her visitor wanted.

'Hello,' he said diffidently, 'hope you don't mind – I was passing and, well, I have a question and I hoped you might be able to answer it.'

The young woman smiled. 'Well, I'll try.' She put out a hand to shake. 'I'm Miss Goddard, I'm the village school teacher.'

'Oh, yes. Sorry, how rude of me not to introduce myself. James Astley. I'm staying at Breydon Hall for the Christmas celebration.'

The woman seemed slightly perturbed by that but she carried on smiling.

'And what is the question with which I may help you?' The voice was polite though he thought it a touch guarded. It was a very proper voice; the diction was perfect and from her accent he concluded she was not local.

'I was wondering about the children?'

She paused, clearly considering her response. 'About what, in particular, were you wondering?'

'Oh, only that there don't seem to be any in evidence in the village, you know, playing snowballs, building snowmen. I thought perhaps they were still in school – but ...,' he waved a hand around indicating the emptiness of the room, '... it seemed strange.'

She again smiled but he didn't feel she was at ease. 'Well,' she said, 'the school is closed for the festivities so that is why we are empty here.' She paused as if considering what would come next. 'This is a small village; there are not many children in it. My class is very small. It is possible many of them have gone away for the Christmas holiday. I do not really know the answer to your question – I'm relatively new in my post. I'm from Cambridge.'

Astley nodded, 'That's a long way off.'

'I was offered the position not much more than a year ago. I was to have been the governess to Lady Pamela's ward, Eleanor Boyes – you must have seen her if you are staying at the Hall with Sir Anthony. When I arrived I was instead asked if I would run the village school. They had lost their old mistress some time back and there had been no school for some little while.'

'I think I have seen the girl – but I've not met her. Does she have some kind of mental deficiency?'

Miss Goddard looked taken aback by this. 'Good lord, no. Whatever made you think that?'

Astley shook his head. 'Just that she seemed to be having some kind of fit – last night – there was a bit of a commotion at the Hall, poachers or intruders of some sort; not quite sure really but it seemed to set her off – that's all. Do you have many pupils at the school?'

Again she looked slightly out of sorts and hesitated. 'No, it's a small class: Maisie Fendyke, Miss Eleanor, there's John Handley, the old mill owner's grandson; his mother died in the birth and then the father died in an accident two years later. The grandparents brought him up but now Handley himself is dead I don't know if John will come back. There are one or two others, not many; people have been moving away from the village.'

'Why would they do that?'

'That is something you would have to ask them,' she said curtly. 'I am afraid I cannot help your further.' And with that she indicated the conversation was closed.

He left the schoolhouse and went directly to the chemist's shop. The chemist was a doleful-looking man wearing the white coat of his trade. His frame was spare and bony, his body tall and gangly and his features sharp, giving him the look of a ferret. He was, however, pleasant enough and served him affably, but when Astley mentioned casually the absence of the children and wondered where they were the chemist's reaction seemed strange. He leaned close to Astley.

'Well, if we knew that,' he said in a hushed tone, 'that would be another thing altogether.'

The response surprised him but before he could question it, the chemist withdrew to the back of the shop, declining to say more. Having wrapped the purchases in brown paper, and tied them with string, he handed them over.

'That'll be one shilling and tuppence, sir.'

Astley paid the man and left. On his walk back he mentally raked over the last two days and puzzled over them. Passing the Breydon Arms he remembered he still had the key to Handley's mill. He had decided not to go back there again; the incident with the car almost coming to disaster in the dyke and the encounter with that peculiar woman had rather put him off. He would take the opportunity to return the key to George Wolston and if he wasn't there then he would leave it in the care of the landlord.

Inside, the pub was quiet; people were elsewhere, still about their business. He looked around for George Wolston but there was no sign of him. There were two or three men hanging round the fire hearth, warming themselves, indulging in slow conversation while they smoked their clay pipes. The rich smell of strong tobacco hung in the air. He went to the bar and asked the man behind it if he was the landlord.

'That be me,' he said, in the lilting local accent. 'How is it oi can help you, sir?'

Astley placed the large iron key on the counter top. 'It's the key to Handley's mill. I wonder if you would be good enough to give it to George Wolston when he next comes in.'

The landlord took down one of the pewter tankards that were ranged in a row at the back of the bar, each one with a name engraved on it. He dropped the key into it. 'This'll be George's,' he said, then hung it back on its hook. 'Eel ave to moind e don't swallow it with ees next ale. Was you a thinking about buoyin Handley's then, sir? 'Cos if you were there's things you need to be a knowin' about that place.'

Astley laughed and shook his head. 'Good grief, no; I just used it yesterday. I was looking for bitterns and you get a good view from the top of it. I must go. Thank you, landlord.' He wasn't halfway to the door when the landlord's words caused him to stop. He went back to the bar. 'What did you mean when you said there were things I should know?'

'Just there's been strange goins on – they do say the old place is cursed.'

Astley indulged a short laugh. 'Oh, come on, man. You don't believe in that kind of mumbo jumbo surely – this is 1927. Next you'll be telling me there are ghosts.'

The landlord shrugged, 'Ave it your way. Still, it's no matter if you're not a buoyin it. Good day to you, sir.'

He waited until he got outside then half out loud said, 'Superstitious clap-trap. This is an age of science not myths and magic.'

As he passed by the schoolhouse on the other side of the street the front door opened and Miss Goddard stepped out onto the pavement. Seeing him she waved and made her way over to him. 'Mr Astley, I think I owe you an apology.' She coloured up a little and her cheeks went a shade of pink.

Astley was taken by surprise. 'Whatever for?'

She fidgeted awkwardly with the bag she was carrying. 'I was rather abrupt with you back in the classroom. I thought I might have offended you and I wished to say sorry.'

Astley put up both hands in protest, 'My dear Miss Goddard, there is no need I assure you.'

'You asked about the children,' she went on, ignoring his remark. 'There is something strange. When I first came here there were nearly twenty children in the classroom.' She paused and looked around as if she might be overheard by some passer-by. 'Now we are down to a less than half.'

'How do you explain that?'

'I don't, I can't, and when I ask I am fobbed off with some paltry excuse about people moving away.' Once more she looked about her. 'I have seen the parents of these missing pupils; they have not moved away.' A note of suspicion had crept into her voice. 'And here is another thing. As we approached Christmas this year the classroom was even further reduced. The children simply disappear and the parents will not be drawn on it. As at the moment we broke up for the holiday I had been reduced to no more than Maisie Fendyke and Miss Eleanor. Two pupils, Mr Astley, ten per cent.'

Astley was transfixed by what she had to say. 'Have you any idea why this is?'

She raised her shoulders in a hunch then let them drop. 'No, not the slightest idea, but even more curious,' she dropped her voice to a whisper, 'I have heard a rumour that these children have been taken for a purpose.'

'And what purpose would that be?'

She shook her head vigorously. 'I wish I knew, Mr Astley, I wish I knew. Whenever I ask questions it's as if the whole village closes ranks on me. It can be quite intimidating.'

Astley thought for a moment. 'Well,' he said finally, 'I could ask. Sir Anthony probably knows something. There's bound to be a rational explanation, you know – there usually is.'

When he arrived back at the Hall he was greeted by the spicy smell of mulligatawny soup. It was lunchtime and he was famished.

CHAPTER 6

The missing and the lost

'That's a damn curious thing.'

Astley held up a newly developed print which he had just picked out of the tray of fixing fluid with a pair of tweezers. In the subdued light he could make out the marshland scene he had taken from the balcony of Handley's mill. It was one of the frames with the woman standing among the reeds – except she was not alone. There were others behind her, shadowy and indistinct but they were there. How could he have missed that? The light was still good when he shot the frame. He placed the second exposure he had taken into the developing fluid and watched as the picture he had taken of the woman emerged. Slowly and indistinct at first, but as the black and white image became stronger it was clear that she was alone, the other figures were missing. He floated the print into the fixing tray and agitated it for a few seconds before hanging it up with the other one to dry.

He took the prints down from where they hung; they were still slightly moist but he was now in a hurry so he patted them dry with his handkerchief before slipping them into a brown paper envelope. He looked at his watch; it was almost half past two. The day was running out; it was the afternoon of the day before Christmas and soon everything would shut, but now he had an urgent errand.

'Are you orf somewhere, dear boy?' the Brigadier called as he came out of the library and into the hallway.

'Need something from the village,' Astley shouted back as he disappeared through the front door. Outside he climbed into the Lagonda. The cold engine turned sluggishly and at first he thought it was not going to start. He pulled on the choke lever; that did it and with a kick the engine shuddered into life.

There was still snow on the roads as he made his way to the village square. When he reached the Breydon Arms he skidded the car to a halt, jumped out and went straight inside. The bar was deserted. He went to the counter and called out, 'Shop!' There was no reply but he could hear the sound of a voice coming from behind a door. He walked over to it. The door had a hand-painted sign that read 'Private.' He rapped on it with his knuckles and waited. The door opened and a young woman's face appeared.

'I'm looking for the landlord.'

She shook her head, then pushing past him went round behind the bar. 'He's gone to Yarmouth.' She fixed him with a suspicious stare. 'How did you get in here anyways? If it be a drink you're after we're closed till six.'

'The door was open and, no, I don't want a drink. What time is the landlord back?'

'Not till late, ees gone to one o' them licensed victuallers association meetins. Oim the barmaid, oi shall be owpnin up ternoit.'

He was on the verge of leaving when a thought came to him. He pulled the photos of the woman out of the envelope and placed them on the bar. 'Do you know who this woman is?'

The barmaid leaned over them. 'I knows her. Where'd you get them from now?'

'I took them, yesterday, out by Handley's mill.'

'Well, oi never. She's not bin in these parts for a while oi'll say.'

'But who is she? Do you know?'

'A course oi do – that be the old schoolmistress. She left the village a woil back. Some do say there was a scandal, though I don't know what. Oi think it was in the Yarmouth Merc'ry. I heared she went funny in the ed.'

'How long ago was that?'

'Can't rightly say. You could try asking the Merc'ry; they got an office in the town just across from the Regal cinema. Why'd you wanna know?'

Astley grabbed the photos and took off, shouting his thanks as he went. It was nearly three o'clock, Great Yarmouth was only a ten-minute drive and the office should be open until five.

He found the offices of the *Yarmouth Mercury* just where the barmaid had said, opposite the Regal cinema. Inside he found a receptionist; she was sitting behind a polished wood counter reading a copy of the paper's evening edition. She smiled at him affably. 'Good afternoon, sir. How can I help you?'

Astley pulled out the pictures. 'Your newspaper covered a story on this woman a while ago and I was hoping I might be able to get hold of a back issue.'

The receptionist stood up. 'I'll see if I can find someone on the editorial to help. Do you know when we ran the story?'

Astley shook his head. 'Fraid not.'

The receptionist hesitated. 'That might be difficult without a date, sir, but I'll ask.'

A few moments later she returned accompanied by a middle-aged man wearing a waistcoat and a shirt with a celluloid collar. He had a pencil tucked behind one ear and ink stains on the first two fingers of his right hand.

'Ronald Tollmache, editor. How can we help?'

'James Astley.'

The two men shook hands. Astley handed the photos to the other man. 'I understand the *Mercury* ran a story on this woman some years back. She was the schoolmistress over at Breydon – some kind of scandal I am led to believe. I wondered if you could trace it for me?'

Tollmache screwed up his face in a grimace. He pulled a watch on a chain from out of the breast pocket of his waistcoat. 'We close in less than two hours,' he said dolefully. 'I'll see what can be done, but you'll understand – it's Christmas, everyone wants to get home. Wait here, I'll ask around. The senior reporter is still here; he probably would have covered it.'

Ten minutes passed then Tollmache returned together with another man. 'This is Fred Haines, our senior reporter. You're in luck; he remembers this story. It was a while back though.'

Haines offered a hand to shake. '1921 to be precise. Remember it well. Emmaline Davis, that was her name.' He picked up one of the photos. 'Extraordinary, she's been missing for years – and you say you took these a few days ago?'

'Yes, out at Handley's mill. I was out there trying to photograph bitterns.'

'What was it about?' Tollmache queried.

Haines thought for a moment. 'Can't remember precisely. I seem to recall she'd secretly had a child – not married. She'd managed to keep it hidden for about three or four years but somehow it came to light. When it was discovered the parish threw her out of her post as schoolmistress and the lodgings that went with it. They took her child from her; that was probably the last straw, poor devil. It was widely thought she'd drowned herself. There was someone who said she'd thrown herself into the dyke over at Handley's mill. There was a search for her but no body was ever found.'

Tollmache looked confused. 'But you say you saw her by the mill.'

'Actually, I first came across her *in* the mill – but when she saw me she ran out of the place. She seemed shocked to see me there.'

Haines was shaking his head. 'Well, I never; fancy you seeing her like that. I've heard reports of sightings before – only rumours and the story isn't that interesting any more – but if you're willing I'd like to use one of these pictures to do a little follow up story. If you don't mind, that is.'

'Yes, of course. She must have taken to living in the mill, I suppose – but if she's as distressed as you say might it not be better to leave her in peace, poor woman?'

'We'd pay you for the photograph – and your story,' Tollmache added quickly.

Astley looked uncomfortable at the suggestion. He wasn't keen to get involved with local gossip; it somehow felt like a betrayal of his host's generous hospitality. 'I'll think about it,' was all he said.

On the drive back to the Hall his mind churned with what he had heard. It was a most curious situation and he contemplated the idea of digging his way to the truth of the matter, though he was not sure how it would be received in the village. If Haines' recollection was true then there was probably an unwelcome taint on the community which nobody would want to resurrect. He toyed with the idea of raising it with the Brigadier but he was unsure of how it may be taken.

When he arrived back at the Hall the afternoon was pretty well spent. There were lights on in the house and as he stepped out of the Lagonda he saw Morton coming up the drive hefting a huge holly wreath on his shoulder, which he took into the front porch.

'Would you be a holdin' this for me now, Master James?' He indicated the wreath, which he then lifted and handed to Astley without waiting for a reply. With a hammer he drove a nail into the oak front door.

'You just hook him on there,' he nodded at the nail. 'Tha'll be doin just foin.' He stood back to look at it and in that moment of pause

Astley decided Morton might be as good as anyone to ask about the schoolmistress.

'Morton – what can you tell me about Emmaline Davis?'

Morton Wolston seemed to consider the question for a few seconds. His face was set with a serious expression. 'Well, now, Master James, oi can't rightly say. How do you mean?'

'She disappeared, didn't she? She had a child and it was taken away – isn't that so?'

Morton's face hardened. ''Tis best not for you to question the ways of the village, Master James. No good'll come of it and that's certain.'

Astley felt flustered and irritated at the evasion. 'I don't understand it,' he snapped back at him. 'What is it you people are trying to hide?'

Morton moved closer and lowered his voice. 'There were things, things that was not roit, that should not have bin – and there are still things that are still not roit; but oi shan't be a messin' with that, Master James. It's not for me – if it's answers you'll be wantin then you'll best ask Sir Anthony; but if you take moi advice you'll leave things be. Now oi'll bid you a good afternoon and you have a pleasant Christmas.'

The response was not what he had been expecting. In truth he wasn't sure what he had expected. He had blundered into something that clearly wasn't his business, and it was obvious from the guarded way everyone responded to him that there was a secret hidden in this small village community, a secret that perhaps should be respected. But he could not bring himself to abandon the pursuit of its discovery. However, the prospect that he might upset the Brigadier and, worse, Lady Pamela gave him pause for thought.

It was while he was sitting in his room that he heard it. He was immersed in a book and at first didn't notice. Then it came to him. It was that song again, the one the woman had been singing when he disturbed her in the mill. Someone was singing it close by – out on the landing. The voice was sharp and high-pitched like that of a child. He went to his bedroom door and opened it, just pulling it ajar. He could hear the words clearly this time

Following, following always to roam;
Following, following leaving your home.

GIRLS AND BOYS COME OUT TO PLAY

Follow the music that leads you away;
Hoping you'll come back one happy day.

Climb up the stairs and into your bed;
Pull up the blanket and over your head.
Don't hark to the music or you will be led
To the place where you stay until you be dead.

Following, following, list'ning too long;
Following, following, things do go wrong.
Over the marshes and far, far away,
Maybe you'll come back, one happy day.

Don't follow the music, don't follow the song.
Stay safe in your bed till the morn' comes along.
Don't follow the piper for he'll make you pay,
And you'll never come home though your mothers do pray.

He pressed his ear closer to the gap. There was a lull, then the voice started to sing the rhyme again.

Stealthily he pulled the door further ajar. When there was sufficient room for him to pass through the gap he stepped out into the corridor. It was empty, but he could still hear the strains of the voice, still singing. It had to be coming from the rooms above. He went as quietly as he could along the corridor to the landing and then up the stairs to the next floor. As he stepped into the dimly lit corridor he came face to face with the singer; he recognised her instantly – it was Emmaline Davis. For a moment he stood transfixed just staring at her. Recovering from the shock he took two paces towards her and, clearing his voice, asked her directly, 'What are you doing here – are you invited?'

Emmaline Davis said nothing in reply. She simply smiled and, passing him by, made her way to the landing and disappeared down the stairs.

Then he was aware of a pounding noise coming from the end of a corridor, fists banging on wooden panels and then a long brittle screaming. He went quickly in the direction of the sound, which was coming from a room that he calculated was the one occupied by Eleanor, Lady Pamela's ward. So distressed was the noise she made that he felt compelled to do something, anything to help. He put his face close to the door and called out to her. 'Are you all right in there? Can I do anything for you?' He listened, but the room had gone silent. He tapped lightly on the door.

'Can you hear me? Is there anything I can get for you? Miss Eleanor?'

Then he heard it, a mournful sobbing and the stuttering words of the song, half sung, half spoken. The girl in the room was singing it; then she fell silent. He waited for a bit then tapped on the door. 'Miss Eleanor, are you all right in there?'

Eventually he gave up; the thought that now pressed on him was that he ought to let someone in the household know that Emmaline Davis had somehow come into the house. He was sure that she should not have been there. Why should she? She was hardly likely to be a guest at the Hall, not if as the reporter from the *Mercury* had stated she had left under the cloud of shame. He went back along the corridor to the landing and then down the stairs, all with a sense of urgency. If she had crept in through the kitchens unseen, who knew what she might be about.

He found the Brigadier in the dining room discussing the cellar requirements for the evening meal with Parkinson.

'Sorry to interrupt, Sir Anthony, but there's something you ought to know.'

The Brigadier broke off his instructions to Parkinson and waited till the butler had left the room. 'Go on, my boy, what is it?'

'I think there is an intruder in the house.'

'Intruder – what sort of intruder, dear boy?' The Brigadier smiled broadly as if he were dismissing the idea lightly.

'A woman. I saw her go down the staircase.'

'Sure it wasn't Mrs M?'

'No, no, sir. It was not Mrs M; this was a young woman.'

The Brigadier's smile darkened. 'Hmm, what was she like this young woman?'

'I think I know her, sir, I think it was the village schoolmistress – the old one, Emmaline Davis.'

The Brigadier's face now looked hard and humourless. 'What would you know of that woman? How would you know her? You haven't been listening to village gossip, I hope. Not prying, dear boy, are you – into village affairs? I shouldn't like to think you had. I shouldn't like that at all – not good form, you know.'

'Of course not. I just happened to come across her out at Handley's mill.'

'Well, leave it with me.' The Brigadier's voice was abrupt and he ended the conversation with the statement that he would go and look around the house. He left the room shouting, 'Parky, Parky, where are you, man?'

By five o'clock the sun had set and the light was gone. A fog had risen from the damp of the marshes and when he went outside to get the photos he had left in the Lagonda the first thought that struck him was how quiet the night was. That was short lived; from around the back of the house the noise of an engine hiccupped into life, the steady plod of its exhaust note interrupting the tranquillity. It left him wondering for a moment and he went off to investigate. In a small shed on the edge of the kitchen garden he found the answer; someone had just kicked the generator into life – and in that instant all around the Hall Christmas lit up. He poked his head round the half open door and looked into the shed. Morton was wiping down the green-painted donkey engine with a rag of cloth, running his hand over it with the loving care of an engineer.

Astley rapped on the door to announce his presence and was greeted by a happy smile. Morton lifted a hand and cupped it to his ear, then leaning close to the engine listened to its steady beat. Happy that all was as it should be he stood there admiring it for a moment. Ever since the Brigadier had installed the generator Morton had considered it his baby and treated it with the same care he would a child.

'She'll keep the Hall bright,' he grinned. 'Thar's one choild that'll not go a missin' Christmas.' Then he indicated with a wave of his hand that they should leave the shed.

Back outside in the quieter air, with the sound of the engine shut in, it crossed Astley's mind to mention the intruder, thinking perhaps Morton might be more forthcoming with an explanation than the Brigadier.

'I saw the strangest thing just a while ago, Morton – inside the Hall,'

Morton had already started to walk away from the shed and in the direction of the tied cottage where he lived. He stopped in mid stride and looked questioningly at Astley.

'There was an intruder, a woman. I saw her on the stairs; she was right at the top of the house. When I told the Brigadier he dismissed it, which is strange because I'm sure she had no business there. I think it was that schoolmistress, Emmaline Davis. I'm sure it was her.'

Morton hesitated, then turned and headed for the driveway and the lane that would take him to the village. 'Oi have an errand for you, if you'd be so good, Mister James.'

'An errand?'

'Now, oi'd be obligated if you'd tell the Brigadier I have gone to the sexton's house.'

'Of course, is it important?'

'It is, so if you'd be over there quick now oi'd be grateful, sir.' With that, Morton disappeared into the night.

It was Lady Pamela he found first, coming out of the drawing room.

'Oh, Lady Pamela, do you know where I can find Sir Anthony? I have a message from Morton Wolston.'

She smiled, 'Is it important?'

'Morton thought so. He said to tell Sir Anthony he's gone to the sexton's house. Isn't that Ralph Fendyke, the sexton – that is?'

The smile vanished. 'He's with Eleanor; she's had one of her turns. Don't worry, I'll see to it that he gets the message right away.' With that, she went directly up the stairs calling over her shoulder, 'Don't worry, I'll tell him.'

Astley stood there for a moment, unsure of what was going on or whether he could do anything. Then he remembered the photos, still sitting in the Lagonda. Having retrieved them, he went to the laundry room where he had left the rest of his pictures drying. Mrs M had taken them down and set them neatly on the laundry table. He would, he decided, take them to the library where the electric light was brighter and he could examine them more closely. He was no longer interested in the bittern. Instead he wanted to look again at the image of Emmaline Davis, and particularly at the figures standing behind her – the figures that he had missed but who had been caught by the keen eye of the camera.

In the library he stood in a shocked trance. He had a photograph in each hand and his eyes flicked back and forth between them. He put them down and shuffled the other pictures, then he counted them. He knew how many frames he had shot and they were all there. He held up the two photographs again, eyeing them in disbelief. There were the reed beds with their snow-covered mud banks where she had stood when he took the pictures, one of her and one with the others almost hidden behind her. But now there was something different – she had gone. Emmaline Davis was no longer there; she *had* gone – and with her the others. His first thought was to find the Brigadier and tell him. Then he realised it would be pointless; it would sound as if he were slightly odd. There seemed to be enough odd behaviour going on as it was without him contributing more. Yet he felt compelled to do something or at least talk to someone about it; it was frustrating.

He paced back and forth along the line of bookcases, tapping his fingers on their mahogany shelves. He pulled out odd books in a random action, not really looking at their titles or taking in their subject; just pulling them out, leafing through a few pages then slotting them back into their place. He was not taking anything in; his mind was occupied elsewhere. He pulled out yet another book, opened it and as he did so something between the leaves fell to the floor. He bent and picked it up.

It was a photograph, which by its pose had been taken formally, probably by a studio. He supposed someone had used it as a bookmark then forgotten about it. He was in the process of putting it back in its original resting place when he noticed there was something written on the back. The writing was faint and he had to hold it up to the light to read it. It was short: 'Thank you for a lovely day dear Ratty, your adoring Em'. He smiled, 'A *billet doux*,' he said under his breath, closed the book and put it back. No sooner he had done that when another thought crept into his mind. He took out the book again, this time examining the picture more closely. It was a woman, probably no more than twenty years old, with her hair piled up into a loose Pompadour with a flowing curl languidly trailing around one cheek. The mouth and the pose were discreetly seductive but it was neither of those that caught his attention. It was the face; it was Emmaline Davis; not as old as the woman he had encountered at Handley's mill and again on the stairs, but it was her, of that there was no mistake. He felt a shiver across the back of his neck as if something had brushed against it.

Dinner was served at eight but the atmosphere was strained from the beginning. The Christmas lights in the dining room were merry enough and the guests were at pains to admire them, but there was a tense atmosphere. It began with the arrival of the first guest shortly after seven o'clock. The Reverend Tayborne had walked from the vicarage, a distance of nearly a mile; he came in stamping the snow off his shoes in the shelter of the front porch. It may have been the season of joy and goodwill but the vicar carried a worried scowl on his face. Once Parkinson had relieved him of his coat he disappeared into the library together with the Brigadier. From the tenor of the mumbled voices Astley took the message that something was not right.

Shortly behind the vicar the Pearsons arrived; Bob Pearson was in the dress uniform of his old regiment, the Royal Suffolk Yeomanry. He too joined the conversation in the library. Lady Pamela immediately herded Val Pearson towards the drawing room, scooping up Astley from where he had been loitering near the library. Parkinson, who had gone ahead after disposing of the coats, now presented a tray of cocktails.

'This is interesting.' Val Pearson took a glass, held it up to the light for a moment then took a diffident sip, not sure it would be to her taste.

'It's a Hanky Panky, dear girl – all the rage at the Savoy: gin, sweet vermouth and just a dash of Fernet-Branca.'

Val Pearson turned to Astley. 'Did you manage to track down the shy Bittern?' she asked by way of polite small talk.

'Only one, but I good a couple of good snaps of it.'

'I've told him he should be here in the spring,' Lady Pamela interjected, 'then you'd hear them boom. It is a quite haunting sound.'

'Will your ward Eleanor be joining us for dinner?' Astley thought it an innocent enough question but it dampened the conversation.

'No, she's having one of her turns,' was all Lady Pamela added and the subject died there.

The appearance of the men saved the situation. 'Come along, ladies,' the Brigadier extended an arm to his wife, 'let's get to the dinner table. What are we having?'

'Soup followed by pheasant; I've asked cook to keep it simple tonight. We are bound to over indulge tomorrow.'

'What, no pud?' The Brigadier put on an expression of exaggerated shock.

'Just a blancmange.'

The soup plates had been cleared away and the pheasant served when there was a pop, like a small explosion, and one of the light bulbs overhead burned out. Within seconds another went, then a third. Lady Pamela picked up a small silver bell and shook it vigorously. Parkinson appeared.

'Parky, fetch in some candles will you; a half dozen will do. If any more of these new-fangled globes blow we shall be eating in the dark.' Parkinson lit and arranged the candles in two candelabras, which he placed on the table.

'This is rather romantic,' Val Pearson quipped. 'Don't you think so, darling?' She put a hand on her husband's arm and he patted it.

'We could do with some more electricity in the church,' Tayborne was saying when another loud pop extinguished one more of the globes. Those remaining began to pulsate. Then the fairy lights on the Christmas tree fluttered and went out.

The Brigadier got up from the table. 'Damn!' he shouted, 'Parky!' Within seconds Parkinson appeared with two more lighted candelabras; he had anticipated the need and set them at each end of the room.

'Go over to the tied cottage and get Morton. Ask him to see what's going on with the genny. The current's fluctuating; it's killing all the globes. Hurry along man – and ask Mrs M to find more candles – don't want to sit in the gloom. Need to see what I'm eating.'

A moment later the electricity failed and the house was plunged into darkness. Only the dull illumination from the candles pierced the blackness. Lady Pamela got up from the table. 'I'll help Mrs M. We shall need candles in the hallway and on the landings.'

As she made her way towards the kitchen there was another sound: the muffled banging of hands on wood, then shouting and crying. It was coming from the top of the house and Astley knew exactly where.

'Eleanor,' Lady Pamela gasped, half choking on the word. 'I'll need your help, Valerie. You too, Reverend.' She grabbed a candelabra from the table and headed for the stairs, the other two hustling in her wake. In the same moment the Brigadier rose abruptly from his chair.

'Come on, Bob!' He shouted the words like a man leading a charge and rushed out of the room. Seconds later, Astley saw the two men run past the dining room heading for the front door – each carrying a shotgun.

Alone in the room Astley sat surrounded by silence; after a barrage of noise and frantic activity everything was now quiet. Then, from the far distance, he heard what sounded like a woman's voice. He got up and went over to the windows where he drew back the heavy velvet drapes. Cupping his hands around his eyes to keep out the light from the candles he pressed his face to the glass. He had a clear view out to the edge of the river. There she was, standing among the reeds, her face silver in the moonlight – and she was singing that nursery rhyme.

He stood transfixed both by the sound and the image; it was quite ethereal and he struggled to rationalise what his eyes and ears were recording. Then everything was drowned by the explosive sound of a fusillade of guns being fired. The silence was shattered and he physically recoiled from the window. When the shock subsided he pressed his face again to the glass – the woman had gone. There was quiet again. A short while after that the lights came on, abruptly and without warning, as if the sun had just risen, popped up over the horizon and bathed every corner with its light.

The others then began to return, first Val Pearson, then the Brigadier with Bob in tow, and finally the Reverend Tayborne with Lady Pamela; she looked drawn and anxious but quickly fell back into her role of hostess. She ordered cook to heat up a boat of gravy to revitalise the now chilly food and everyone carried on as if nothing had happened. Parkinson discreetly made his rounds replacing the burnt-out globes.

Astley looked at the assembled company and wondered what if anything he should say. The Brigadier, spotting the questioning look, laughed and shrugged. 'Sorry about the interruption dear boy. Must have shocked you a bit by the look on yer face. Damn poachers.'

CHAPTER 7

The girl in the upstairs room

Mary Wolston went about her chores and began the preparations for their Christmas feast. She had been married to Morton for nigh on fifty years and for all that time they had lived in the little tied cottage on a small plot of land not more than 100 yards from Breydon Hall. They had one son, George, who worked on Curtain's farm in the nearby village of Burgh Castle.

When they first moved there, Breydon Hall had been a working farm and Morton had secured the post of bailiff, but after the death of Sir Arthur Boyes, the Brigadier's father, the farm had been let go and most of the land sold off. Since then Morton had served Sir Anthony as a mend-all and fix-all; he could make or repair most things. His most important role was to keep the newly installed generator running and the house supplied with electricity. Other than that he cut the grass, which he insisted on doing with a sickle even though there was now a cylinder mower; he cut timber for the fires and managed the fruit and vegetable gardens for the Hall kitchens.

There would be just the three of them to sit down for the Christmas lunch and before that they would go to church for the midday service. She had two brace of pheasants, the annual gift from the Hall and a duck from the marshes that George had shot two days before.

'What were that business up at the Hall last noight, Mort? Ha she come back agin?'

Morton shook his head slowly from side to side. 'Same as last year, same as all them years.

'Won't she never give up then?'

'Not till she got what she want.'

Mary placed three glasses on the dining table together with a crystal decanter. 'Come on, George,' she called up the narrow staircase that led to the bedrooms. 'Parsnip woin. The best from last year.' She poured a measure of the pale straw-coloured wine into the three glasses and passed one to Morton. George came clattering down the steps to join them and together they raised a toast. 'To Breydon Hall and our good life; and God bless both.'

'Yer father and me, we was just talking about that ta-do up at the Hall last noight.'

George put on a disapproving look; he screwed up his mouth and shook his head. 'That Master James, he been a proddin' about in the village, askin' questions a folk. I heard the Brigadier were none too happy wi that.'

Mary looked from one to the other of the two men. 'Can't see woi.'

'Simple,' Morton's voice was blunt. 'They'll be a feared a what comes out.'

Back in the kitchen Mary looked out across the meadow that separated them from the Hall. 'Oi just hope she leave em in peace for the day,' she whispered to no one in particular, then began peeling potatoes.

Astley woke to Christmas day, having slept soundly, and was surprised he had done so, his head being that full of the events of the last three days. As he ran his bath he examined what had transpired.

The woman who sang the nursery rhyme was clearly Emmaline Davis, though she seemed to have about her an ethereal air, like that of an old-fashioned spectre from the ideas of years past. This challenged him; he did not like the idea of the supernatural, of the phantoms of his parents' generation. This was, he argued, the age of the internal combustion engine, of electricity, of radio and rational investigation into every phenomenon. Men had mastered the air, they could fly. The men of science had probed in all directions and into every facet of the state of being – but nowhere had they found evidence of those spectres which had haunted our ancestors. She must be mortal, he argued, otherwise why set on her with shotguns. Nevertheless, there was something not quite human about this woman.

What disturbed him more than that was the silence that surrounded these events. He was certain there was a conspiracy to keep a secret from him. He did not believe the story of poachers. Emmaline Davis, he was sure, had some attachment to Breydon Hall, beyond that of being the village schoolmistress, and what was she doing out at Handley's mill – and how did she manage to get out there? There was no omnibus transport, it required a car, or a horse at very least. Unless, of course, she knew some route across the marshland reed beds. That might explain what she was doing out there and how she got to the Hall. The river, he had observed, ran to no more than a muddy stream when it was at the bottom of the tide. There was barely enough water in it to float Morton Wolston's little dinghy. The reed cutters had regular paths through the marsh and she must know them: that was clearly the answer.

Satisfied he had solved that puzzle he dressed and went down to breakfast. Lady Pamela and Sir Anthony were already seated when he entered the dining room.

'Good morning, dear boy, hope you slept well – and a happy Christmas to yer.'

'I did indeed, Sir Anthony.'

Lady Pamela smiled and motioned towards the sideboard, loaded with the morning's offering: toast, tea, scrambled eggs, bacon, black pudding, and some small chipolata sausages. 'Do choose what you would like. Phyllis will serve you.' She picked up the silver bell and gave it a vigorous shake. The girl who came in answer to the ringing was barely out of her teenage years. Astley had not seen her before.

'Phyllis is our maid of all work,' Lady Pamela announced, seeing the look on his face.

'A good girl, this one,' the Brigadier grunted through a mouthful of sausage and toast. 'Bin with us for five years now – isn't that right, Phyllis?'

The maid bowed her head politely. ''Tis right, sir.'

'Bin visiting her parents; gave her a few days orf. She's not from around here yer see – are you, Phyllis?'

'No, sir. Gorleston.'

'Gorleston, yes – now see to Mr Astley here.' He spiked a piece of black pudding onto his fork and stuffed it into his mouth.

'Will you accompany us to the Christmas service, James? Parky'll drive us to the church in the motor; snow's gone slushy, can't let the memsahib get her shoes all mucked up. Tubby Tayborne does a good Christmas service – plenty of tradition and carols, don'tcha know.'

Sir Anthony's motor, a Daimler Landaulette, was parked close to the front of the Hall with Parkinson at the wheel. The day was fine with a blue sky overhead and he had dropped the rear hood down so that the passengers in the back could benefit from the bracing air – though he had carefully left the windows wound up so that Lady Pamela's hat and veil would not be disturbed in the slipstream. The silent sleeve-valve engine was running with barely more than a gentle hiss. Lady Pamela, Sir Anthony and James Astley were driven the short distance to the church in a stately progress, waving at those struggling on foot to the service.

Inside, the church was lit with a glorious array of candles, spangling their light off the altar silver and the polished brass plates commemorating previous generations of the worthy and the important. A garland of ivy had been laced around the small pipe organ together with wreaths of holly. But, for all its lights, the church was cold and as the parishioners stood to sing the first hymn, wrapped in their warm coats and scarves, streams of condensation came out of their mouths, draping the words of praise in a ghostly breath of fog.

As they walked up the aisle to the family pew at the front of the church Astley caught sight of the schoolmistress, Miss Goddard. Their eyes met and Astley acknowledged her, nodding in her direction. Her face creased with a tentative smile.

The service was long and tedious. The Reverend Tayborne intoned his way interminably through the order of service, studded with interludes of carols and backed by a droningly long sermon. By the time the last carol had been sung and the final blessing received Astley was beginning to wish he had not agreed to attend. However, as he came out through the church porch and waited for Lady Pamela and Sir Anthony to greet other members of the congregation he found himself standing next to Miss Goddard, and this brightened the moment.

'Have you noticed,' she said quietly, 'that there were no children at that service? Now that is a curious thing for a Christmas Day, don't you think?'

'It had not escaped my attention – and, yes, that is curious.'

'There's something else I thought you should know. I found this tucked away in a cupboard at the school.' She reached into her handbag and withdrew a small bundle of letters tied with a ribbon.

'What are they?'

Miss Goddard looked furtively about her. 'Letters – of a very personal nature – put them in your pocket – and quickly.' She again turned her head left and right. The congregation was slowly filing out but Lady Pamela and the Brigadier remained inside.

'I don't like to pry into private letters but …,' she dropped her voice to a mere whisper. 'They are love letters – from someone calling himself Ratty – to Emmaline Davis.' Her voice hushed to an even lower whisper. 'It may be that whoever wrote them was the father of her illegitimate child.'

Astley looked puzzled. 'So why give them to me?' Miss Goddard shuffled uncomfortably and appeared slightly embarrassed.

'When you came to the school yesterday I thought you seemed interested in her – that's all.'

'Any idea who Ratty was?' She shook her head.

The appearance of Sir Anthony a few moments later brought the conversation to a close. Astley took his leave of her and joined the others who had now climbed into the Daimler where they waited for him. 'Jolly good service,' he remarked to Astley, as he installed himself in the comfort of the leather upholstery. 'Take us home, Parky.'

They arrived back at the Hall and tramped in through the front door where they were greeted by the exotic aroma of a stuffed goose roasting on a spit in the kitchen. The Brigadier took a hold of Astley's arm and steered him in the direction of the library. 'Come along, my boy, let's have a snifter to the get the celebrations started. A quick whisky before the others get here.'

'That's an interesting portrait.' Astley pointed towards a painting that hung over the mantle of the fireplace. 'Formidable looking character, if you don't mind me saying.'

The Brigadier guffawed and handed Astley a glass. 'Lord Rattigan, my grandfather, made his fortune in Rhodesia – tobacco and gold; great friend of Cecil Rhodes, you know. My side of the family were Rattigans when you go back a generation. My mother married into the Boyes. That's where the name comes from. Anthony Baverstock Rattigan Boyes. Terrible mouthful; all got shortened when I was at school. Went to Rugby – the other scallywags called me Ratty.'

Astley almost dropped the glass he was holding and for a brief moment a wave of guilt flowed across him as he remembered the letters hidden in his pocket. He felt like a sneak thief in the presence of his victim, caught red-handed with the loot. He downed the whisky more quickly than was seemly.

'You all right?' the Brigadier asked. 'You look as if you've seen a ghost. Here, let me give you a refill.'

The clock in the hallway chimed the half hour: two thirty. Astley excused himself and went to his room. He took the packet of letters from his coat pocket, untied the ribbon and opened the first one to hand. It was dated January 1918 and it was clear from the postmark that it had been sent through the BEF Army Post Office in France. There was no indication of the sender but the letter was addressed to Miss E Davis, Breydon Village School; it was signed 'your own true and loving Ratty'.

By the time the Christmas dinner was announced he had read all he needed to read. Leaving his room he heard what he took to be the voice of Eleanor calling from the floor above. He had solved one mystery, the lover of Emmaline Davis, but he was still left wondering what the story was behind Eleanor's incarceration. He supposed she must be mentally deficient in some way though Miss Goddard had said no – or perhaps she was a sufferer of the epilepsy condition. That, he had heard, brought on fits.

CHAPTER 8

Closure

They sat down to the Christmas feast at four. It was, Astley thought, an irregular hour at which to dine. It was too late for lunch and too early for dinner. Outside the light had gone and the house now glowed with the brightness of the electric lamps. The Christmas tree in the dining room, the third in the house, was a kaleidoscope of iridescent baubles. Fragile glass figures of Saint Nicolas, candy canes and brightly coloured birds were hung in the branches of the tree; and draped across it all, a long string of fairy lights.

They were six at the table. The vicar had been the first to arrive, followed closely by the Pearsons.

Phyllis brought in the first course: a silver tureen of mulligatawny soup, bright yellow with turmeric and mildly spiced. Next to each diner she placed a small dish of chilli sauce. 'Make it as hot as ya like,' the Brigadier cheered as he upended the contents into his soup dish. 'Got a taste for the old chilli pepper in India; dashed good.'

The Reverend Tayborne cleared his throat. Sir Anthony, who had started to stir the chilli into his soup, stopped. 'Ahem,' he muttered and waited.

Tayborne looked briefly around the table. 'Shall we bow our heads while I say grace?' The ritual prayer over, the room filled with the sound of spoons clattering on dishes and soup being sipped and slurped.

Next there came a terrine of creamed sole dressed with a lobster bisque. Valerie Pearson went into raptures over it. 'Pamela, you really must let my cook have that recipe – it's divine.'

The goose made its entrance on a huge silver trencher carried aloft by Parkinson. It was placed in front of Sir Anthony who stood up and, coming stiffly to attention, saluted the roasted bird. 'Old regimental tradition, James,' Bob Pearson said, leaning across to address Astley. 'Does it every year. Won't let Parky carve till he's honoured the fowl.'

Parkinson picked up the trencher and removed it to a sideboard where he proceeded to carve and plate the feast, directing Phyllis to carry each loaded plate to the guests. Finished with that procedure, he went round the table with a claret jug for the men and a sweetish hock for the two women.

The talk at the table was dominated by Sir Anthony and Bob Pearson who regaled the company with anecdotes from their time in India and then the Great War. The women were politely bored and Astley made a determined show of his interest, though he was finding it less than fascinating. As he sat listening and watching he wondered what it was Emmaline Davis had seen in what was turning out to be a rather boorish man. He was viewing the Brigadier in a new light.

The overhead lamp flickered; then it went out.

'Not another globe gone.' There was a sharp note of exasperation in her voice as Lady Pamela looked up to the ceiling. A moment later it came on, flickered some more and then steadied.

'Why does it do that, Anthony!' It was less a question than an indication of her annoyance.

They finished the meal with a boiled fruit pudding, round as a cannonball and cloaked in flaming brandy, a sprig of holly poked into the top, and draped with a thick yellow custard. Finally a ripe stilton cheese was ported ceremoniously to the table, accompanied by shelled walnuts and batons of skinned celery. It was, the Reverend Tayborne declared, a feast to remember.

The light flickered again and once more went out. This time it stayed out. Lady Pamela got up from the table. 'Come along, there's no point sitting here in the dark. We should all go into the drawing room. Parky can get Phyllis to light some candles and put them in there as well – in case it all fails again. It is so unreliable this electricity.'

'James, my boy,' the Brigadier put a hand on Astley's arm as they all trooped towards the drawing room, 'pop back into the dining room, will ya. Fetch in that port decanter. It's a good half full and Parky's gone orf to find a few candles.'

With the aid of the light in the hallway he could see into the dining room and the dim shape of the decanter still sitting on the table. As he entered he encountered Phyllis who was coming in through the service door to the kitchen. She was holding a lighted three-branch candelabra. Seeing him, she let out a short involuntary shriek.

'It's only me,' Astley said defensively.

'Oh, sir, you gave me quite the shock.'

Astley retrieved the decanter. 'Didn't mean to frighten you.'

Phyllis laughed nervously. 'Sorry I screamed sir – it's just…' she paused as if uncertain, '… it's just there's a lot of things that's weird about this place. I shan't be staying – I'm telling you.'

'Weird, what sort of things?

'Well, there's that poor girl locked up in that room for one.'

'And?'

Phyllis shook her head. 'I don't like to say, sir, t'would be unlucky to talk of it; but just you listen to that.' She held up her hand and in the moment of silence that followed he heard it: a child's voice was singing. Phyllis put down the candelabra and throwing a glance over her shoulder, hurried back to the kitchen.

He stood in the gloom and listened. There was no mistaking the rhyme; it was more of a chant than a song. A chill ran across him as he went to the window and stuck his head through the gap in the heavy velvet drapes.

With no light behind him and a full moon in the sky he could see clearly out across the grounds to the marshes beyond. There was no one – and the singing had ceased.

Out in the hallway the electric lamp failed. It did so without the sound of a switch or the pop that usually accompanied the failure of a globe burning out; the light simply ceased. Astley picked up the candelabra that Phyllis had left on the table and, holding it aloft and with the port decanter in other hand, he made his way through the gloom to rejoin the others.

In the dining room the air felt brittle. The fire was blazing but the room felt cold and there was a silence that hung over everyone. From the hallway there came the faint movement of light as Mrs M set down another candelabra on the hall table.

The Reverend Tayborne got up from where he had been sitting in a soft leather sofa and, holding up one hand as if to command silence, walked quietly to the window. In the same moment there was once again the sound of that hauntingly childlike voice and the words of the nursery rhyme. The fairy lights on the Christmas tree now fluttered like a trapped butterfly in a spider's web. Then everything went out and they were left with only the soft light of the candles. Tayborne wrenched apart the curtains and there she was. It was unmistakably Emmaline Davis. Her face was pale and her hair hanging limp around it looked damp and tangled. The vicar lurched back a pace and then, holding up the crucifix which hung on a chain around his neck, began to mutter an urgent incantation.

'Parky,' the Brigadier bellowed as he jumped to his feet, 'look to the girl. Come on, Bob, she's back. I'm damned if I'll let her get away with this.'

As he headed for the door Mrs M appeared with a pair of shotguns. The men grabbed one each. 'James,' the Brigadier shouted over his shoulder, 'find Morton and get him to the generator – she's bloody well stopped it again.' With that they were gone. As he made his way through the kitchen and out through the back door he heard the cries of what he took to be Eleanor and the muffled banging of her fists on the solid door of her room.

Out in the night air under the light of the moon Astley headed for the Wolstons' cottage. It was not far and the pale glow of its oil lamps through the small windows marked it out plainly. He rapped hard on the door.

When Morton saw him standing there it was plain he knew what was happening.

'It's that woman,' Astley blurted out. 'She's sabotaged the generator. Brigadier wants you to get it going again.'

At first Morton said nothing, only beckoning Astley in with a nod of his head. In the single room that served the cottage for all its functions George was already up from the table and on his feet. 'Oi'll be needing you, George.'

The two men left without further word, leaving Astley standing in the room with no other company than Mary Wolston. He stood in dumb silence, looking at her and wondering what he should say about his rude arrival at their table.

'She'll not give up till she has them all.' Mary Wolston slowly shook her head. 'T'aint roit what she be doin – but t'aint roit how she was done by.'

'Do you know what's going on?'

'Acourse, and so do everyone in this village.'

Astley held out his hands in a gesture of exasperation. 'I don't understand why nobody will tell me what this is about.'

'Half is cos they feels frighted by it – and half is cos they feels guilty; that's why they won't say nothin'.'

Astley smacked his arms against his sides like and angry bird, 'I don't understand. I know Emmaline Davis was Sir Anthony's lover and I heard there was a child. Is that what this is about?'

Mary Wolston pursed her lips; a grave expression spread across her face. 'There was a child. He treated her roit bad. Poor woman thought he'd do roit by her and she'd marry and be mistress at the Hall.'

'He abandoned her?'

'Worse than that. When he come back from the war he took the child and she were thrown out; out of her employ at the school and out a her lodgin. She were turned out at Christmas.'

Astley looked shocked. 'That's appalling.'

'He sent her away and he gav her money to stay away. So long as she kept quiet and away from the village he would keep a roof over her head. But she pined fair to sick for the child and eventually she could take it no more – so she drowned herself – out there – on the Breydon marshes.'

Astley said nothing as he listened in near disbelief.

'But that's only the half of it.'

'Go on.'

'Afore she killed herself she vowed she would take all the children from the village. None would be spared. The Parish and its council had taken her child – and now she would take theirs in revenge.'

Astley huffed out a long slow sigh. 'And that's why there are no children in the village.'

'Every Christmas she's bin back and taken what she could. After the first ones were lost, those as could they took their children and left them with friends and relations – outside the village and as far away as they could. There's only two left now and she won't rest till she has them all.'

He shook his head in slow realisation at what he was hearing. 'Little Maisie Fendyke,' he said quietly, then in an urgent voice went on, 'and who is the other one? I've only seen Maisie.'

'Why – Miss Eleanor, of course, their love child, the one what started it all.'

'My God.' Astley slapped a hand on his forehead. 'Of course, that's why she's locked away. What a terrible existence.'

'Oh, she's not always locked away like that. Only at Christmas when her mother comes calling; standing there in the Breydon marshes singing her awful song. It's like a charm, you see – and those little ones are drawn to it.'

'What happens to them?' There was the ring of incredulity to his words as he struggled with the tale Mary Wolston unfolded.

'She keep 'em with her, tha's what. Into the marshes, no one ever sees them agin.'

'And she's back – for the other two.'

''Tis so, she's back, like last year and the year before.'

Astley fell silent again, his mind whirling with the information. Then it dawned on him. 'Hang on a minute. You said she committed suicide – drowned herself on the marshes, you said?'

'Well now, that be roit enough.'

'But that can't be. I've seen her; I saw her out at Handley's mill and again in the marshes – and just tonight up at the Hall, standing outside the window.'

Mary Wolston raised her eyebrows and shook her head. 'Only a spectre, Master James, just the troubled soul of that poor woman. That's what you seen. She be no more than a ghost.'

Astley thought on it. 'No,' he eventually said, 'that can't be right – else why shoot at her with shotguns?'

'Well, as my Morton do see it, he says she just be a miasma and the shot disturbs its formation. He thinks the blast blow it away like the wind does with a mist. I don't rightly know now, but tha's what he says.'

'Listen.' Astley moved abruptly into the kitchen and opened the back door. The muted sound of firing came to them on the night air. 'Thank you, Mary, I must go. I have to see this thing for myself.'

He listened for the direction of the shooting but inside he knew where he would find them. Down by the bank of the river a group had gathered. The tide had run out and there was no more than a trickling stream in the middle of a swamp of black mud that was the river bed. Bob Pearson, Morton and George Wolston were repeatedly discharging fire at a figure on the far bank. In the river mud the footprints of a recent crossing glistened under the moonlight. Two of the group, a man and a woman, were down on their knees crying. Between the rounds of gunfire Astley caught the distinct and eerie call of the unmistakable chant. The man on his knees was Ralph

Fendyke. 'She've taken Maisie,' he said in a cracked, broken voice, then sank back into sobbing.

The spectre of Emmaline Davis wavered and began to dissolve. The men put up their guns and waited. A deep silence descended, broken only by the sobbing. 'We need to get across and find Maisie,' Bob Pearson said, peering out over the marsh.

'You'll not get across the mud,' George Wolston warned him. 'You sink in that. That'll not support more than the weight of a choild. We can get the dinghy in when the toid come up.'

'We have to do something ...,' but Bob Pearson was cut short. On the far bank the miasma of Emmaline Davis reformed. Astley was transfixed by the apparition, but it was not alone. Standing close to it, the shadowy form of a child, its hand held in the clasp of the spectre stared at them across the muddy abyss. The child was Maisie Fendyke. They both began to sing the nursery rhyme chant. Alice Fendyke rose to her feet and let go a long, hollow moan of despair. It was the end of her child.

In the same moment there was a high-pitched scream from behind the group and the figure of Eleanor burst out of the darkness. Behind her the voice of the Brigadier bellowed like a bull in full anger. 'Grab her, someone. Stop her!'

George Wolston dropped his shotgun and, with a sideways lunge, caught the girl by her shoulder, swinging her round until he wrapped her in a bear hug. Eleanor screamed at him to let her go, kicking out with her legs at him. A few seconds behind her the Brigadier and Parkinson ran breathlessly to the edge of the bank; a moment later Tayborne arrived, panting like an exhausted dog. They stood on the bank while the vicar, once more holding up the cross of his faith, called out to her to let the child return and to go to her rest in peace. Neither the spectre not the child paid any heed. They continued to sing and the effect on Eleanor was manic. Her fury rose and, in a whirlwind of kicks and screams, she bit George Wolston in the hand. He let go and as she fell from his grasp she scrambled down the bank and onto the mud of the river bed.

Where Maisie was barely six and as light as duck down, Eleanor was now twelve and too much for the mud to support. As she began to sink Sir Anthony threw aside his shotgun and jumped down into the slurry of black ooze; his legs were immediately sucked down but his life as a military man had made him strong and he had dealt with mud like this in the trenches of the Great War. He had seen how men could save themselves by throwing their bodies out flat across the slime as if they were swimming. With careful movement, not too rapid or agitated, a life could be saved.

Dragging himself to where Eleanor had become engulfed, he took her arms and slowly pulled her free from the sucking morass. Onshore someone had brought a rope and now they threw it out to the victims. He tied it in a loop around her and up under her arms. 'Get the girl out!' he yelled. Slowly they hauled and slid the limp body of Eleanor across the mud until she was back on the river bank. She was exhausted but alive.

In the middle of the river Sir Anthony waited while the lifeline was again thrown out to him. But the effort of pulling Eleanor's imprisoned body free had come with a cost and now his body replaced hers as it became trapped in a sticky grip. The men ashore lined up like a team in a tug-o-war. Fishermen used to hauling in nets, they slowly inched his body away from the mud's lethal embrace.

On the far shore, seemingly floating on the reed bed, the image of Emmaline Davis waxed and weaved but the song it sang no longer had its effect; Eleanor had ceased struggling and instead stood close to the others, staring across at the miasma of what had been her mother. The men on the rope had come to rest.

Bob Pearson looked down from the bank. 'The tide is coming up,' he said anxiously. 'We have to get him out or he'll drown.'

The men got back onto the rope and inch by inch the body of the Brigadier came free. On the far side the miasma was now waving and swaying from side to side, changing and rechanging its form; the song gave way to an anguished calling as Emmaline Davis tried to reclaim her daughter. It sighed and moaned, 'Eleanor, Eleanor, come back to me.'

Eleanor looked around her at the others, then took a step closer to the river's edge. She held out her hands towards the ghost. 'Mother,' she called, her voice soft with a quiet emotion, 'let the children go. Let them free and I will come to you. Me for them, Mother. If you want me back you must let them return.'

From his prison in the mud the Brigadier let out an impassioned cry to his daughter. 'No

Eleanor, no. Please not that. I beg of you. Eleanor.' His voice changed to barking diatribe as first he shouted abuse at the spectre; he accused his lover of selfishness, of lusting for revenge on him by taking the life of their daughter, of having no love for anyone but herself. But the ghost of Emmaline Davis was not to be placated and it continued to stretch out its arms and beckon with siren calls.

'Give up the children, Mother,' Eleanor's voice was cracked with tears and laced with pleading, but it was clear she was no longer under the spell that had taken the others. The truth was that in the moment of her rescue she had ceased to be a child and had become an adult.

The spectre seemed to waver. The image waxed and seeing it the Brigadier began to shout; all reason and rationale had deserted him. 'Leave the girl, she has a life, she deserves to live it. If you want revenge then take me – if indeed you have the courage.'

At this the spectre seemed to settle into a state of tranquillity. It became the clear image of Emmaline Davis once more. Then, as if by a miracle and one by one. the faces of the lost children appeared from behind the apparition.

First to come across the treacherous mud was Maisie Fendyke, with the others in a crocodile file behind her.

Brigadier Sir Anthony Boyes untied the rope that encircled his chest and let the loose end drop from his hand. As the tide rose to cover him, the spectre of Emmaline Davis settled itself next to him – and then he was gone.

When the tide next fell those who had witnessed the end came down to retrieve the corpse – but there was no body, nor any trace that one had been consumed by the mud.

Eleanor was free and the village once more had its children.

Two days later James Astley left for London. On the Acle Road he stopped the Lagonda close to the turning that led to Handley's mill. There he got out and, using the telescopic lens, took a souvenir picture. It was all he would take away – that and the story which he decided then and there he would tell to no one, though he would set it down on paper so that in later years if he doubted his memory it would be there.

EPILOGUE

Norfolk 2010

They bumped along what was left of the track, the Range Rover making easy work of what would have been a challenge to an ordinary car. About a mile in they came to an old mill.

'What do you think, Robert?'

He laughed, 'I think it's seen better days, darling.'

The woman sitting in the passenger seat pulled a face. 'Yes, but you can imagine it, can't you? You know, when it was working and the sails were intact.'

She got out of the four-by-four and walked a short distance until she came close enough to reach out and put her hand on the decaying brickwork of the building. Looking up, she saw the remains of what had once been a wooden structure. 'Look here,' she called to her companion, 'this must have once been the staircase, the one he wrote about.' She fished around in her handbag and pulled out her mobile phone. 'Come and see this.' She tapped on the photo icon and flicked through the gallery of pictures. 'There,' she said, as he joined her, and held out the phone for him to see. 'That's his original photograph, the one I found in the exercise book.'

Robert looked up at the mill. 'Do you think the story was true then?'

'I don't know. He was my grandfather but he never spoke about it – at least not to me. Granny Astley once let drop that something like this had happened; she was the schoolmistress, you know. I wish now I had questioned her about it. Her family name was Goddard. That's the same as the one in his story.'

'I think he made it up, Sarah. I suspect your grandfather came up here, got the idea from seeing the mill, and then turned it into a jolly good story that he wrote down in that exercise book.'

She gave him a sly smile. 'You're such a cynic, Robert.'

'It was a compelling read, I grant you, but be reasonable. Who on earth believes in ghosts? I think you could probably get that published if you wanted to.'

'Nope. Come on. Let's go and see who we came to see.'

They drove back along the track to join the A48, what had once been the Acle Road, turned onto it and headed in the direction of Great Yarmouth.

'I think you could be up for a horrible disappointment when this turns out to be no more than a clever confection of your grandfather's imagination.'

Sarah shook her head dismissively. 'Well, we can settle this once and for all when we get to Breydon.'

Robert shrugged. 'We'll see. How old is she now? She must be ancient.'

'Ninety-five; it's a bloody good age. When I spoke to her carer she said her memory was still quite good and she was very coherent considering her age.'

At Gorleston they turned right and followed the signs for Breydon. When they got to the village Robert pulled the Range Rover to a halt outside the Breydon Arms. 'Amazing,' he said in a low voice. 'This is the pub all right.'

'And the church,' Sarah commented, tugging on his arm for attention. 'And look, that's the war memorial, just as he described it – except it's now got the Second World War chiselled into it.'

'Looks like the school's gone.' Robert pointed to a development of small modern houses.

Sarah nodded and waved a hand towards a wine bar. 'I think that might have been the old chemist's shop.'

They lingered for a short while, just looking at what was around them. 'Don't you think it's kind of eerie?' Sarah grinned. 'You could believe it happened here.'

Robert shrugged. 'Quite implausible, darling. Come on, let's go and see Lady Boyes and put a lid on this thing.'

The drive leading up to the front of Breydon Hall was exactly as her grandfather had described, right down to the porch and the oak front door. As he rang the bell Robert put out his hand and with one finger scratched at what remained of a rusty nail – all but corroded away; just a stub iron. 'Well, would you look at that, darling; that could be the nail Morton Wolston hung that wreath on in the story.'

'Not a story,' Sarah grinned and nudged him in the ribs. 'A true account of real events – you'll see.'

The door was opened by a young woman in a nurse's uniform. She looked from one to the other of them, then said in a quiet voice, 'Miss Astley?'

The woman took them through the hallway and into a large room with windows that looked out over the reed beds to Breydon Water. 'If you take a seat I'll bring Lady Eleanor to you – but I must ask you not to talk for too long. She is quite frail now; she had a stroke three years ago and it has taken its toll.'

The woman left and when she returned she came pushing a wheelchair. Huddled into it was a small fragile-looking woman, her hair thin and white, her bony face mottled with the brown marks of age. Sarah stood up and gave a courteous sort of half bow to the old woman, unsure of how she should approach her. The nurse signalled for her to sit down and pushed the wheelchair closer to them. Lady Eleanor's face creased with a feeble smile.

'It is so good of you to see, us Lady Boyes.'

Eleanor made a small tutting noise. 'My dear,' she replied in a husky whisper, 'it's good of you to come and see an old woman like me. Not many do. Now what can I do for you?'

'We wondered if you could tell us something about my grandfather. He stayed here once, a long time ago, when you were a girl. James Astley.'

Eleanor's face brightened. 'Ah yes, James Astley. He was a handsome man, you know. Was he your grandfather?'

Sarah nodded. 'Yes, he knew your father.'

Eleanor thought for a moment. 'Did he – I didn't know that. Were they in the Great War together? That was a terrible war, you see.' At that she stopped and seemed to stare vacantly out through the nearby window.

'No,' Sarah said in a very precise tone, 'he was too young for that. He came to stay here one Christmas – in 1927.'

Eleanor came back to them and again her wrinkled face broke into a fragile smile. 'Oh yes, I remember that. It was a strange Christmas that one.'

Robert leaned forward and looked into her eyes. 'Why strange, Lady Boyes?' She seemed reluctant to answer that and instead went silent again.

'Did something happen?' Sarah felt her pulse rate rise. 'Do you remember?'

Eleanor began shaking her head. 'We had electricity; we were one of the first to have it around these parts. It was wonderful but ...' She faltered again making a humming sound as if she had lost the thread of what she had been saying; she smiled and then chuckled. 'It was so unreliable, it kept going out and every time it did the bulbs popped and had to be replaced.' She giggled some more at the recollection.

They waited patiently to see what else would come, but there was nothing. Sarah felt a pang of disappointment. 'Was there nothing else, Lady Boyes? You see my grandfather mentioned some kind of tragedy.'

Eleanor thought on it, the gentle smile faded and was replaced by something more wistful. 'Oh yes, that's right. There was a drowning in the river. A man tried to cross when the tide was out and he got stuck. Men from the village tried to save him but the tide came up and covered him. They never found the body, you know.'

'Yes,' Sarah tried to disguise her excitement, 'I think that man was your father.'

Eleanor smiled again. 'No, no, my dear. I remember the man, he was from the village – he was the sexton. Yes, his name was

Fendyke, Ralph Fendyke. I seem to recall his daughter had wondered off and got stuck in the mud. He went in to save her. It was no good, of course, you can't get out of that mud. They both drowned, my dear. A most tragic event.'

'Are you sure?' Sarah persisted. 'According to my grandfather it was your father, Sir Anthony Boyes, who was drowned – he was attempting to save you from the mud and he got stuck and was covered by the rising tide.'

At this Eleanor became quite adamant. 'Oh no, if that is what your grandfather says he is quite wrong. No, no, it was Ralph Fendyke and his girl. I remember it clearly.'

Sarah looked crestfallen and it fell to Robert to end the matter. 'Thank you so much, Lady Boyes. You have been most helpful and we are grateful. There is one question I would like to ask though.' Eleanor nodded her consent.

'I know this might sound odd but, well, are there any stories about the Hall being haunted, any stories of a supernatural sort?'

Eleanor looked a little incredulous. 'My dear young man, whatever made you think that?'

'Just a story I'd heard.'

'No, no, I shouldn't like to think that. Oh dear, no.'

Robert stood up and nudged Sarah to do the same. They took their leave and went back to the car.

As the left the driveway, Sarah looked back over her shoulder at the Hall and the marshes. On the distant horizon she could just make out the ruins of what had once been Handley's mill.

'I can see how my grandfather would have been inspired to write what he did,' she said quietly. An air of disappointment hung on her words, and as the Hall slipped from view she settled into the realisation that what James Astley had written was nothing more than a story, inspired by the landscape and the death of the Fendykes. It had, after all, only been a fiction.

When they came to the village square Robert pulled to a halt in front of the Breydon Arms. 'Right,' he said cheerfully, trying to lift her spirits. 'Let's see if we can get some lunch before we head back.'

Inside, the Breydon Arms had changed; it was no longer the place that James Astley would have recognised. The Saloon Bar had been knocked through to join the Public Bar, making one continuous space, half of which had been given over to dining, leaving the remainder scattered with casual chairs and low tables. The players of cribbage, dominoes and cards were long gone as was the darts board, which had been replaced by a television screen hung high up in one corner.

Sarah cast around her with little enthusiasm. 'I suspect this has fundamentally changed since my grandfather came here,' she was saying, but then she spotted the row of pewter mugs hanging along the back of the bar, the same mugs that had been there since who knew when. 'Look,' she said, tugging on Robert's arm, and she pulled him over to the bar where the barman was serving a glass of wine. She waited till the customer had paid.

'I love the pewter tankards,' she said, perking up. 'Are they original?'

'They are,' the man replied. 'They were here when we bought the place. We liked them and thought they were worth keeping. They've all got names on them, you know. My wife says they're the ghosts of old customers.'

'Can you look and see if there is one with the name George Wolston on it – if it's not too much trouble?'

The landlord turned and went along the row of tankards, taking down each one in turn. About a third of the way along he stopped. 'Here we are.' He looked pleased and surprised. 'How did you know that would be there?'

'My grandfather met him once, more than eighty years ago. Isn't that fantastic – it's still here. Do you mind if I take a picture of it? Perhaps with you holding it up?'

'Not a problem.' The landlord lifted the mug but then he hesitated. 'I have a better idea.' He waved to a woman who had just come into the pub and was being helped to a seat by an elderly man.

'She's our oldest customer; she might even have known this …,' and he stopped to read the name on the tankard again, '… George Wolston. Mae, have a look at this.' He came round from behind the bar and led them to where the woman was sitting. 'Did you know this one, Mae?'

The woman opened her handbag and produced a pair of glasses. A toothless smile ran across her face. 'Acourse oi do,' she said in an accent that was fast disappearing from the county.

'That were old George's mug; used it till the day e doid; oh tha' be twen'y years back. Twas im and old Morton helped save Eleanor Boyes when she were no more than a littl'un. She went out on the mud and got stuck fast, you see. She'd a doid if they ha'nt got to her. Course it took her father, though. He just stayed – twas all on account o' that wicked woman.'

Sarah's heart jumped up into her mouth. 'But Lady Boyes told me it was a Ralph Fendyke and his daughter who were lost?'

The old woman let out a derisive 'Ha! What would she know? She's dafter than my old goat.' She shook her head solemnly. 'No, it were the fault o' that schoolmistress. She were dead – but she come back for him. She weren't lettin' him a go, not after what e did to er.'

The landlord was raising his eyebrows and making a twirling motion with one finger around his temple. 'She goes off like this,' he whispered to Robert. 'I shouldn't pay too much attention if I were you.'

Robert ignored the landlord and instead leaned closer to the woman. 'Tell me,' he said softly, 'what was your family name when you were a small girl?'

'Why, Fendyke acourse. I were christened Maisie but everyone call me Mae.'

'Ah,' he said quietly, 'I think that explains everything.'

OTHER BOOKS BY THIS AUTHOR

A Right to Bear Arms   An epic of love, betrayal and the shadows of war. Set in London and New York during 1939–40, the author tries to imagine what might have happened if Britain had done a deal with Hitler and come out of the war. Where would this have left America? The story follows the lives of three couples as they struggle with the prospect of war.

The Girl in the Baker's Van   A romantic thriller set in France during the Second World War. Evangeline Pfeiffer is on the run from the Gestapo; her only hope of escape is to persuade SOE agent Richard Grainger to help her – but Grainger has his own mission.

The Haunting of the Harlequin Goat   A psycho-thriller set in modern-day New York. When psychiatrist Lydia Kroll takes on a new patient she is faced with a dilemma. Is Don Loreto suffering from PTSD hallucinations or is it something far more sinister? As she uncovers his past she is faced with conclusions that challenge her deepest beliefs.

Turn Left at Istanbul The ultimate mad sixties road trip, based on the author's recollections of a real overland journey from London to Calcutta in 1969. A hilarious and irreverent travelogue, wittily told, as he and his companion Douglas bounce from one comical mishap to another, along a road beset with traps lying in wait for the unwary.

More Than One Passion Top American scientist Remington Grove is called in to lead the hunt for a missing Nazi weapons expert and a formidable superweapon. She has been teamed up with British army intelligence officer Guy Blackwood and together they search across war torn Europe. The brief is simple: 'find Kammler before the Russians do.'

Printed in Dunstable, United Kingdom